£3.50

The Grand Duke's Woman

The Grand Duke's Woman

*The story of the morganatic marriage of
Michael Romanoff, the Tsar Nicholas II's
brother and Nathalia Cheremetevskaya*

PAULINE GRAY

MACDONALD AND JANE'S · LONDON

© Pauline Gray 1976

First published 1976 by Macdonald & Jane's
Macdonald & Co. (Publishers) Ltd
Paulton House
8 Shepherdess Walk
London N1 7LW

Edited by Felix Brenner

ISBN 0 356 083136

Photoset, printed and bound
in Great Britain by
REDWOOD BURN LIMITED
Trowbridge and Esher

Dedicated to the memory of my Russian Grandmother, "the bold and beautiful Nathalia Cheremetevskaya", in the hope that some (but not too much!) of her remarkable courage and spirit lives on still at least in her great-grandchildren.

Contents

Prologue ix

PART ONE THE LIFE
1 Natasha 3
2 Michael 13
3 Love 19
4 Marriage 29
5 Exile and Pardon 36

PART TWO THE TIMES
6 Unrest and War 47
7 Rasputin 59
8 Revolution and Abdication 65
9 Vortex 81
10 October and Onwards 89
11 Perm 96
12 Prison and Freedom 105

PART THREE SURVIVAL
13 Aftermath 119
14 Exile – England 131
15 Exile – France 142
16 The End 159
17 Ifs and Buts, and Might-Have-Beens 168

Acknowledgements 172
Appendix – Rumours 177
Bibliography 195
Index 197

Prologue

In Paris, on that afternoon in 1965 it was raining. It was in November, and rain was only to be expected. The passers-by hurried on their way, and the traffic at the Trocadéro was throwing up a fine spray. The passengers in the buses looked gloomily out of the steamed-up windows at the wet streets.

In the Cimetière de Passy, which is on a slight hill at one side of the Place du Trocadéro, a man was walking around the graves as if searching for a particular one. He was wearing a rain-coat which came down to his ankles and which gave him an old-fashioned, 'foreign' look. He wore the collar turned up and a black broad-brimmed hat pulled well down to protect him from the rain. There was something inescapably Russian in his appearance; in fact he was on a visit to Paris from the U.S.S.R.

He stopped beside a grave and stood there looking at it. A plain wooden cross marked the place, in contrast to the other graves in the cemetery which all had magnificent marble statues and monuments. He was just able to make out the name 'Brassow'. For a while he stood looking at the long grass which covered the grave; turned and walked back down the path to the gates. He entered the keeper's lodge, said something to the keeper, then left the cemetery and walked out into the rain and was gone.

PART ONE
THE LIFE

1 Natasha

The night outside is stormy; I can hear the rain beating against the window panes, driven by the strong wind that blows around the house. Inside where I sit I am warm and dry in my comfortable surburban home, and I am reminded of a poem by Charles Baudelaire:

> *Pluviôse, irrité contre la vie entière,*
> *De son urne à grands flots verse un froid ténébreux*
> *Aux pâles habitants du voisin cimetière*
> *Et la mortalité sur les faubourgs brumeux.*
> *Mon chat, sur le carreau cherchant une litière. . . .*

But my cats, my two Siamese, are lucky and they are here beside me in the warm, and they do not have to scratch at hard tiles to make their bed. They sit in comfort in their favourite chair and watch me with their bright blue eyes a-slant, and from time to time their ears twitch at the sound of the wind and rain outside. I hear the sound of a jet passing high overhead, and then the sound of a car in the street; it stops and I can hear people running from it to reach the shelter of their home. Then all is quiet once more, and I pick up an old photograph out of a cardboard box and look at it. It is of a man and a woman; they sit side by side holding hands. The man, handsome, is wearing a kind of military uniform; the woman, beautiful, is in furs and a hat and white gloves, and she has the saddest eyes that one could ever see. There is something very touching about the way her white-gloved hand is clasped in his, and it is as if they were showing the world that they dared to love each other. And, indeed, that is just what they were doing, for this is a picture of the Grand Duke Michael Alexandrovitch, the younger brother to the Tsar Nicholas II of Russia, and the woman whose hand he was holding so tenderly was my grandmother. Theirs was a romance that caused, in its time, almost as much scandal as did that of the Prince of Wales and Mrs Simpson. For though Nicholas II is known and remembered as the last Tsar of Imperial Russia, he was the last Tsar who was actually crowned, but he was not the last one altogether. It is easy to forget that his brother Michael became Tsar after him, albeit for a very short time, but Emperor he was nevertheless, and my grandmother was his wife. This then is her story and the story of her Misha and of their love; it is the story of those times and how history was against them right from the very beginning and how they never could have had any hope or any chance for a normal life together. And yet hope played a large part in her life.

There are those people who believe in the influences of the planets on our lives, and that our destinies and characters are already written because of the positions of the stars at the moment of our birth. When my grandmother was born in Moscow on 27th June 1888, the Sun was in Cancer and the Moon in Aquarius; according to astrologers this meant that she was going to be, among other things, shrewd, resourceful, sensitive, protective, detached, courteous, and imaginative.

Be that as it may, Nathalia Sergeievna Cheremetevskaya certainly had a stormy childhood. Her father, a successful Moscow lawyer, doted on her, and this caused some friction and jealousy with her two older sisters, Vera and Olga. I will never cease to regret that I paid so little attention to my grandmother when she used to tell me about her childhood, but I do remember some of the things she told me. I know that Vera was greatly admired for her personality and intelligence, that Olga was pretty and had an extremely sharp wit, and though she did not say it outright, I gathered from my grandmother that she herself was the beauty of the family and had the gift of always looking elegant. The three sisters attended a day school not far from their home, and Natasha was often in trouble with the teachers over disciplinary matters, not over her lessons which she found quite easy. At home, after they grew too big to be looked after any more by a fat peasant nursemaid, they had a French governess whom they teased shamefully. Though Natasha was her father's pet, she adored her mother, but admitted to me that she and her sisters would sometimes drive their poor Mamma quite frantic by incessantly arguing and bickering among themselves.

When I knew my grandmother she was an elderly lady, with beautiful snow-white hair, terribly sad eyes, and a lovely face. She was also very gentle and soft-spoken, modest and seemed to have a retiring nature.... When she was young, she had, of course, the same eyes and the lovely face, but that is all. From what I hear, she was a termagant; arrogant, selfish, impatient, intolerant and vain. It was these very characteristics that helped her withstand the troubles and worries that were to be hers for most of her life – troubles and worries that were sometimes of her own making, but more often were simply the workings of Fate. And of course Natasha had courage. That no one will dispute.

So she and her sisters grew up in Moscow. Their life was full and interesting; the political disorders which had already started were confined to the students and workers and did not touch the Merchant Class, to which the Cheremetevskys belonged. This part of Society, at any rate, devoted themselves to the arts in their leisure hours. They attended Moscow's magnificent state-supported theatres, and discussed the varied repertoire of opera, drama and ballet. Every theatre and concert hall was filled to the brim for first nights, and after the performance, practically the only subjects of conversations in drawing rooms and restaurants were the merits or failings of the latest production.

Moscow then had a kind of cozy appearance with its countless churches, crooked streets and busy crowds. The Kremlin was open to everybody, the churches were full, and on every holiday the air resounded with the ringing of hundreds of church bells. Only in Moscow could one feel the impressive contrast between carnival, when the whole population gorged itself on food and drink and the streets were filled with merrymakers, and the beginning of Lent, when suddenly, as if by magic, everyone became still and the church bells tolled majestically calling people to repent and to prepare themselves for the Resurrection. After seven weeks of Lent came Easter, which one could celebrate in the Kremlin itself where crowds of people would wait for the first peal of the great bell of St John's Church. Processions of priests and singers moved around each of the four cathedrals in front of the palace, and suddenly at midnight the great bell began to boom over the whole of Moscow, joined after five minutes by innumerable bells throughout the city.

And then there were the winters . . . the cold nights, and the sound of the crisp snow under the feet; the sight of the main palace of the Kremlin with its dull gold-coloured cupolas shimmering in the moonlight, vividly recalled the old Russian legend about a city full of churches which was said to have suddenly appeared from a lake where it had been submerged and lost for years.

The Cheremetevskys spent each summer at their wooden dacha at Pushkino, a town on the railway just thirty kilometres from Moscow. There were two rivers there, and the girls were allowed to bathe when the weather was hot enough. Pushkino was full of dachas owned by well-to-do Muscovites who spent the summers there, as indeed was the whole of the area surrounding Moscow. Natasha loved Pushkino, and she never forgot her happy, warm summer childhood days spent there.

So the years passed by and in no time Natasha was sixteen and the young men calling were not there for the sakes of Vera and Olga only, but also for the big blue eyes of the young Natasha. One of her school friends had a brother called Dimitri who fell in love with her. Many years later he wrote about her in his memoirs:

> . . . There was a friend of my sister, a charming girl, whom I met at that time. Her blue eyes were appealing and my desire to see her became stronger and stronger, but it never went further than holding hands while listening to

the Tchaikovsky overture to *Romeo and Juliet*. I did think for a while that she was the only girl who could make me happy, but her life took such an extraordinary turn . . . that I did not deem myself good enough to change the course of her life . . .

But Dimitri Abrikossow was not the only man who was susceptible to Natasha's beauty. Among the others was one who was different from the rest; he was older for one thing, and much more serious. His name was Sergei Mamontoff and he had a slight stutter which Natasha secretly found rather attractive. He was already making a name for himself in the musical world of Moscow, and he was about to be promoted to the post of Director of Music at the Bolshoi Theatre.

The Mamontoffs were quite a well-known family in Russia at that time. They owned a factory which specialized in the grinding of colours for paints, and in the manufacture of sealing-wax. They were great patrons of the Arts, and bought many paintings of the French Impressionists at a time when these were unknown in Russia, and they also encouraged Russian painters and sculptors. It was a Mamontoff who heard a peasant singing in a field one day and realized that the bass voice had very exciting qualities; and it was this Mamontoff who encouraged this peasant to come to Moscow to have his voice trained, and who paid for the lessons. This peasant's name was, of course, Chaliapin. There is even a railway station named after the family. Sergei had been coming to the house for some time now, and it was thought that he was courting Olga. Natasha liked him very much; he seemed so sensible and quiet, so different from most of the young men who strutted around showing themselves off like peacocks.

One day Natasha decided to herself that she would like to marry Sergei; she thought that it would be amusing and would astonish her family who all believed that Olga would one day be his bride. She succeeded so well with her plan that it was not long before Sergei proposed marriage to her, overwhelmed and transported by her beauty and charm; and it was a very proud Natasha who took him to see Papa to ask his permission as she was still only sixteen. Papa was unwilling at first, but eventually agreed as he could refuse his youngest daughter nothing. Olga was mortified, but Natasha was thrilled at the idea of her future as a married woman; she was looking forward to getting away from the restrictions and discipline at home, to becoming the mistress of a house and of having her own servants to order about.

To begin with, the marriage was a great success and when she gave birth to a daughter on 15th June 1903, both Sergei and she were very happy and proud. Sergei insisted on naming his daughter after her beautiful mother, and so she was named Natasha as well, but as she grew up and started to talk, she was unable to pronounce her name and called herself 'Tata' instead. This nickname stuck and she was never called anything else by her family and friends for many years.

At first Natasha was thrilled with her role as a mother and wife; she adored watching Nyanya, the peasant nursemaid, as she gave the baby her bath, and she would hold out the warm towel for the dripping infant, and help to dry her. But soon her interest palled and Tata was looked after almost entirely by Nyanya. Natasha became bored with motherhood and marriage. The novelty of being in charge of a house and servants of her own had worn off.

When Tata was two years old it was 1905, a year of unrest and political troubles. Natasha welcomed the tension and excitement as it relieved the monotony of her days. One day there was a rumour that all the water supplies were going to be cut off, so she ordered her servants to fill all possible receptacles, including the bath, brim-full with water and to leave them filled for some time. This rumour turned out to be false because water continued to flow from the taps as usual. On another occasion the family took refuge in the bathroom for one whole night; they had heard the sounds of distant shooting, and as the bathroom was the only room which had no outside window, Sergei had insisted that the family stay there.

When things settled down once more, the boredom seemed even greater to Natasha, and she complained increasingly to Sergei. His reaction was to spend even more time at his work at the Bolshoi in order to escape her nagging. He had been a good and kind husband to her, and he adored his little daughter whom he spoiled even at that early age, but he was of a retiring nature and he could not cope with his wife's outbursts. His instinct was to bury himself even deeper in his work. He had never enjoyed going to parties and receptions, and now he made the excuse that the pressure of his work precluded attending these functions. It is not really surprising that Natasha started to go out without him, often accompanied by an admirer from her youth. His name was Liolocha Wulfert, and he was a handsome young captain in the Blue Cuirassiers. When he was in Moscow he always seemed to find the time to escort her when she went shopping, visiting friends, or to parties.

Natasha and Wulfert enjoyed flirting gently with each other. The old sparkle returned to her eyes and the two young people were often to be heard laughing gaily together. As time went by however, Wulfert became more intense. He had become infatuated by this beautiful capricious creature and was obsessed by the idea of making her his mistress. It was no longer a laughing matter for him. At first Natasha laughed at him, but soon she was overcome by his passionate love-making and could no longer resist – indeed she did not want to resist any more for she was by now in love too, and so she became his mistress.

Natasha was not, even then nor ever, the sort of person who could live her life in lies and deceit for any length of time. She confessed her sins to her husband. She told him that she had not meant to fall in love; that she had just thought to amuse herself as she was bored, but now all she wanted was to remake her life and marry her lover. Sergei was heartbroken. Nevertheless he eventually agreed to a divorce, and in due course when the legal formalities were sorted out Natasha left Moscow with Tata and Nyanya and went to live with her new husband at Gatchina, two miles outside St Petersburg.

Gatchina was a charming small town full of pretty little houses set in the middle of parkland dotted with many lakes, it was a summer resort for the people of St Petersburg. It resembled Windsor, in being both a garrison town and a royal residence, and it was there that the regiment of the Blue Cuirassiers had their headquarters. The Colonel-in-Chief of the regiment was the Grand Duke Michael Alexandrovitch, the Tsar's younger brother.

The days passed most pleasantly for Natasha. Their new flat was always full of handsome young men in uniform, and of course there was the usual social life that surrounds a Guard's Regiment. Natasha was very happy. She had bought some lovely new clothes and she enjoyed showing them off at parties and receptions. With Nyanya there to look after Tata, Natasha was free to enjoy herself to the full. After the dull life she had led in Moscow with Sergei, this new routine was like champagne to her and it went to her head a little. She was radiant and adored receiving admiration, her beauty and elegance were the subjects of conversation wherever she went.

A month or so after Natasha's arrival at Gatchina, there took place a grand Reception, and Natasha was presented to the Grand Duke, her husband's Commanding Officer. As she curtseyed in front of him, she risked looking at him and she felt a thrill as she saw him gazing at her very intently. My mother always maintained that it was at that very instant that Natasha decided to make him fall in love with her, that it would be amusing to win the heart of the brother of the Emperor. Whether that is true, I do not know, but at any rate the Grand Duke lost no time in inviting Natasha to be his partner in the Mazurka, and later took great care to stay at her side for the rest of the evening. Robert K. Massie, in his book *Nicholas and Alexandra* writes: 'Within a few months Nathalia managed to become Michael's mistress. From that moment on, she dominated his life.'

2 Michael

The Grand Duke Michael was a tall, slim, handsome young man. He was the third son of Alexander III and his Danish-born wife Marie. There were two sisters, Xenia and Olga, the latter being four years younger than himself and with whom he was very close. Nicholas was the eldest son, and from birth had been heir to the throne. The second son was George. The possibility that Michael might one day be Heir Apparent was not even considered. He was spoilt as a child and greatly indulged; no one minded or was jealous; everyone loved 'Misha' as he was called by his family. On reading *The Last Grand Duchess*, the Memoirs of the Grand Duchess Olga Alexandrovna by Ian Vorres, one reads of the happy carefree childhood led by the two youngest children of Tsar Alexander III, Michael and Olga. They had an English nanny called Mrs Franklin who ruled the nurseries in a thoroughly British fashion, and she stood for no nonsense from her charges; the fact that they were a Grand Duke and a Grand Duchess made not the slightest difference to her. The children were brought up on a very plain diet, as were countless children in countless nurseries ruled by British nannies. They had porridge for breakfast which Nana had taught the cooks to make properly; mutton cutlets, peas and baked potatoes for lunch; jam and bread and butter and English biscuits for tea; cake was a treat and was only served on special occasions. Olga was the baby of the nursery, and as Michael was that much older he was allowed to come and go more freely, and the other children were allowed to visit the nurseries as long as they respected all Nanny Franklin's rules and regulations. When Olga was seven years old and Michael eleven, the dining-room was turned into a school-room for them. They had lessons every day from nine o'clock in the morning until three o'clock in the afternoon. Michael and Olga became very close as they had such a lot in common; they liked the same people, shared the same tastes in so many things, and they never quarelled. Olga had several special pet names for Michael, her favourite one being 'darling Floppy'. Later on in life when they had both grown up and were perhaps attending official functions, Olga would surprise people greatly by calling out to her brother and calling him 'Floppy'.

Part of their education consisted in dancing-lessons which they hated. The dancing master, Mr. Troitski, was a very dignified old gentleman with beautiful white whiskers, and he always wore immaculate white gloves. He insisted on having a huge vase of fresh flowers standing on the piano for each lesson. Michael and Olga had to bow and curtsey to each other before starting to dance the *pas de patineur*, the waltz or the polka; they knew that despite their orders, the Cossack guards outside the ballroom were watching them through the keyholes, and this made them feel foolish and very self-conscious. After the lessons, the Cossacks would greet them with broad grins and laughter which only served to increase their embarrassment. But they looked forward to their Russian History lessons as they felt that they were learning about family matters, and so it was not just dull, dry history for them.

As Olga and Michael grew older, they were allowed to dine downstairs with their parents and their older brothers and sisters as well as any guests that there might be. Being the youngest they were served last at table, and as in those days it was considered bad manners to eat quickly, they only had time to swallow a few mouthfuls before their parents had finished their entire platefuls and had signalled the servants to clear away the course. As Nanny Franklin disapproved of eating between meals, Olga and Michael were frequently hungry.

Their father, Tsar Alexander III, used to take the two of them for walks. They would set out for the deer park like the three bears in the fairy story – the biggest one in front with the biggest spade; then followed the middle-sized one with the middle-sized spade; last of all trotted the littlest one with the littlest spade. They each carried a hatchet, a lantern and an apple. In winter, Alexander taught them how to fell a dead tree and how to clear a path through the snow and how to build up and light a fire. They then would roast the apples, dampen down the fire and return home by the light of the lanterns. In the summer, their father would teach them how to row.

From time to time the whole family would go to Denmark to visit the King and Queen, the parents of the Empress Marie, the children's grandparents. On some occasions more than eighty of Europe's royal personages used to sit down to dinner at Fredensborg. Olga and Michael would be brought in to say goodnight to everyone before dinner and then if they could they would tiptoe from their bedrooms and peer over the bannisters at the assembly downstairs. In the autumn the favourite dish served on these occasions was roast pheasant, and the children used to sniff the delicious odours. To Olga and Michael, there were other odours as well; to them the English royalty smelled of fog and smoke; their Danish cousins reminded them of damp, newly washed linen, and they thought that they themselves smelled of well-polished leather.

When Michael was about ten years old he was given his first rifle as a Christmas present. The next day he shot at a crow which fell to the ground, wounded. Michael sat down and cried. But in later years he took shooting lessons from an excellent teacher and became a crack shot, but he preferred to use his skill against vermin rather than in sport.

In his book *Nicholas and Alexandra*, Robert K. Massie writes:

> Like many another youngest son and younger brother of a reigning monarch, Michael was ignored in public and indulged in private. Even as a child he had been the only one able to tease his redoubtable father, Alexander III. A family story told of the morning that father and son were strolling in a garden when the Tsar, suddenly angry at Michael's behaviour, snatched a watering hose and drenched his son. Michael accepted the dousing, changed his dripping clothes and joined his father at breakfast. Later in the morning, Alexander got up from his desk, and, as was his habit, leaned meditatively out of the window of his study. A torrent of water descended on his head and shoulders. Michael, waiting at a window above with a bucket, had had his revenge. Grand Duke Michael, ten years younger than Nicholas, grew up a handsome, affectionate nonentity. Although from the death of his brother

George in 1898 until the birth of his nephew Alexis in 1904, Michael was Heir to the Throne, no one seriously considered the possibility of 'darling Misha' becoming Tsar. It was unthinkable. . . .

Michael grew up and entered the army and eventually became Colonel-in-Chief of the Blue Cuirassiers. He was given a country estate of his own called Brassowo, a day's journey from Moscow. It was his delight to immerse himself in the business of running this large estate. In 1901, during a family holiday at Sorrento in Italy, he fell in love with a young lady-in-waiting to his sister Olga, Alexandra Kossikovsky, nick-named Dina; they even planned to elope together, but his mother, the Empress Marie, found out about it all. She gave Michael a scathing talking-to and made him feel thoroughly ashamed of himself; Dina, she sent away as fast as she could, and so the affair died.

That same year Olga had been more or less forced to agree to announce her betrothal to Prince Peter of Oldenburg, a man some fourteen years older than herself, whose parents were intimate friends of her mother. In July she married him. Her wedding night was spent alone, frightened and in tears while her new husband amused himself all night long at his club at his favourite occupation – gambling. Olga wrote later in her memoirs:

> I shared his roof for fifteen years, and never once were we husband and wife.

It was five years later, when he was twenty-eight years old, that Michael attended that fateful reception in his capacity of Commander-in-Chief of the Blue Cuirassiers, and watched as Natasha curtsied in front of him. It was his *coup de foudre*, the lightening bolt that strikes one time in our lives. The gentle young man who once had wept for the death of a crow fell headlong in love with the beautiful wife of one of his officers; a woman who, before arriving at Gatchina had already broken one husband's heart. 'Dear darling Floppy' was in love again, but this time it was more serious and this time his love was to last for the rest of his life.

3 Love

From what my grandmother told me, I gathered that at the beginning of their love affair that it was Michael who was the more deeply in love. He was the one who did the kissing while Natasha proffered her cheek to be kissed, to paraphrase an old French saying. But it was not long before Natasha was as much in love with Michael as he was with her. At first she had been very flattered by the attentions of the Grand Duke. It had been most amusing to seduce the brother of the Tsar (or to let him seduce her). A great many people knew about the affair, and as word of it spread she was recognized and talked about and sometimes even envied. She became even more arrogant than before, and at home was quite impossible. She made Nyanya's life a misery by shouting at her more than ever. As for Tata, when she saw her mother approaching she would run and try to hide somewhere; she was frightened of Natasha's new imperious voice which always seemed to be echoing around their apartment.

But gradually Natasha fell really and truly in love with her Grand Duke. His deep love for her touched her; his gentle character and his quiet passion overwhelmed her. He was so handsome, so tall and slim, with the minute Romanoff waist, and his eyes were blue and clear and his hair was so fair. So their relationship moved into a new phase. He could not bear to let her out of his sight for longer than was absolutely necessary. He began to invite both Natasha and her husband to be his guests in his private box at race meetings, for example; he felt that it was better to see her, even if it meant inviting her husband as well, than not to see her at all. But the scandal was all the greater because of this; tongues wagged away excitedly at the sight of Natasha and her husband in the Imperial box, chatting amiably to the Grand Duke.

As for poor Liolocha Wulfert, he did not know what to do about it. He was in a most difficult and unenviable position. Michael was not only his Commander-in-Chief but the Tsar's brother. Wulfert decided to take the easy course and do and say nothing. He hoped that it would all blow over soon. Meanwhile he would make sure that everyone could see him smiling at the Grand Duke in the usual polite and friendly fashion, and he would go out of his way to be gallant and attentive to his wife in public. Perhaps this would confound all the scandal-mongers and stop the tongues wagging. So when Michael visited their apartment quite often, Wulfert managed to greet him and welcome him. Sometimes Michael would bring presents for Tata. One night he woke her up in the middle of the night in order to give her an enormous peach. As she lay in bed eating it, she felt that Grand Dukes were surely gods to be able not only to produce a peach in the middle of the night, but also actually to allow it to be eaten in bed!

So Michael and Natasha came to love each other so much that they could not envisage life apart. It was Michael who mentioned the possibility of marriage. To begin with neither took it seriously, it was just a word, a thought; it meant happiness and being together for ever, and was wonderful to think about. But Michael persisted; why not? Why should they not marry? Natasha asked him whether he did not care for his position in Society, his army career, because if he married her all these things would be ruined. Michael tried to put her mind at rest. He told her that he did not care very much for his army career, and that in order to marry her he would be only too happy to retire from public life, which he hated anyway, and that they would take Tata and go and live at Brassowo and spend the rest of their lives there in peace and harmony. Natasha began to envisage what marriage to Michael would mean, for perhaps it could really be one day . . . what a marvellous thing . . . what would her sisters say? . . . But there was Liolocha, her husband, to think of, to get rid of. Wulfert, who, not so long ago had seemed to her to be the very acme of her desire had now become the selfish despoiler of her ambitions. The sight of her husband became more and more intolerable to her, and there were terrible and frequent rows. Wulfert eventually agreed to a divorce and one day left the matrimonial home to live in the officer's mess. Natasha's sister Vera had married a clever lawyer called Alexei Sergeievitch Matveiev, and Natasha delegated him to attend to the legal business of the divorce. Often she had to go to Moscow to talk to Matveiev about it all and on these occasions she used to stay in her old home with her parents. Michael would join her when he could for the weekend. Natasha's father, Cheremetevsky, pretended to be ignorant of who Michael actually was and insisted in treating him as an ordinary person. Michael, never before having stayed in an apartment with a simple family, seemed to enjoy the lack of ceremony immensely.

One day Michael wrote to his brother the Tsar asking for his permission for his eventual marriage to Natasha, and begging his blessing. Nicholas was outraged. '. . .I will never give my consent . . .' he wrote to his mother, 'it is infinitely easier to give one's consent than to refuse it. God forbid that this sad affair should cause misunderstanding in our family.' Even so, Michael and Natasha refused to let their disappointment overcome them too much and they continued to spend as much time together as they could. Did they really expect the Tsar to give them his blessing? It seems such a naïve hope that it surely must have been Michael's idea. He must have believed, as all lovers do, that just because his love seemed to him to be the most perfect and exquisite of women, that everyone else would think so and love her as he did.

But one member of his family was warm and sympathetic, and that was his sister Olga. She herself had been living a loveless marriage with Prince Peter of Oldenburg, and as the years went by, had become more and more unhappy. One day in 1903 she had driven from Gatchina to watch a military review at Pavlovsk. As she stood talking to some officers, she had noticed a tall, fair man wearing the uniform of the Cuirassier Guards, and he was talking to her brother Michael. Suddenly he turned and looked at Olga. Their eyes met.

> It was fate. It was also a shock. I suppose on that day I learned that love at first sight does exist.*

Olga let her brother know just how she felt about this

---

* *The Last Grand Duchess*, The Memoirs of the Grand Duchess Olga Alexandrovna by Ian Vorres.

man, and Michael understood and immediately asked the officer, whose name was Nikolai Koulikovsky, to a luncheon party for the next day, and asked Olga to attend as well. The party was a great success and Olga returned home deeply in love, knowing that her feelings were reciprocated. She went immediately to find her husband who was in his library. She told him that she had met a man whom she could love, and she asked him for a divorce. Prince Peter would not consider a divorce for the sake of his family name and his own dignity as well, but he said that he might reconsider in seven years or so. Meanwhile he was quite prepared to appoint Koulikovsky as one of his personal aides-de-camp. So Koulikovsky came and lived at the house, but Olga and he were so discreet in their conduct that no one knew of their love. This *ménage à trois* continued until 1914 when Olga left to nurse the wounded at the Front, and Koulikovsky left to follow his regiment.*

So at the time Michael and Natasha were trying to sort out their love-life, Olga and Koulikovsky used to slip away from the Oldenburg house, and the four of them would go off on picnics together, and a charming photograph of them has survived of one of these occasions. Olga would often drop in to see Natasha at home, and she would turn up dressed very simply wearing a white jersey and skirt with a beret on her head. Once she brought Tata a present of a coral necklace. Captain Koulikovsky was very good at mending broken toys, and Tata considered him a very useful person to know.

Sometimes Michael took Natasha on visits to the

---

* Prince Peter never did reconsider a divorce. In 1916 the marriage was anulled, and Olga and Koulikovsky married quietly.

Tsarski Sad, the Tsar's private gardens. It was really an enormous park which contained all sorts of things to amuse and delight. There was a wishing well into which one was supposed to throw coins and make a wish; there was a tunnel which was said to be a secret passage from the Palace and was rumoured to have been used by Paul I when he tried to escape from being killed on the orders of his mother, Catherine the Great. The whole park was surrounded by a series of lakes which were connected to each other by rustic bridges or small ferry-boats. There were small islands on which were to be found pavillions dedicated to various gods of ancient mythology and a boat-house staffed by a crew of sailors from the royal yacht. It was a most pleasant place indeed.

Occasionally Michael took Natasha on visits to his own apartments at the Palace.

But life was not so pleasant for Natasha outside the privacy of the Tsarski Sad or Michael's apartments. Whenever she went out to the shops, for instance, she would notice groups of women whispering together and staring at her through their lorgnettes; men would leer and laugh together. One evening, at a theatre in St Petersburg with friends, something happened during the interval: an officer in the Blue Cuirassiers whom Natasha had known slightly in the past, went up to her and reproached her in a loud voice for what he termed 'compromising' his Commanding Officer, the Grand Duke Michael. He told her, in front of the crowd which had soon gathered, that the whole regiment felt the same way as he did. Natasha tried to pay no attention, and she walked passed him with her cheeks scarlet with mortification. Later she stormed and wept to Michael.

He was distraught with worry and did not know what to do. One evening, after a long discussion, they decided that the best thing would be for her to leave Russia for a while, at least until the scandal of her divorce from Wulfert died down a little. So, after a passionate and tearful leave-taking Natasha departed, accompanied by an elderly cousin, Katia Froloff, as chaperone, and with Tata, Nyanya and a lady's maid called Anyuta. It was June 1909. They stayed first in Vienna at an hotel, and then made their way to Chexbres, in Switzerland. Michael and Natasha sent each other telegrams, three hundred and seventy-seven of them sent by her. In those days there was no international telephone system, and if people wished to communicate with each other in a more speedy fashion than letters, they used telegrams. Copies and rough drafts of some of these have survived; some are in English, some in French, and others are in Russian. They make touching reading. I am so glad that Michael and Natasha were unable to telephone each other so that these scribbled messages of love exist to this day.

It was not long after Natasha's departure from Russia that Michael started to plan a journey to Copenhagen, ostensibly to visit his mother's relations, but really in order to meet with Natasha; this was to be their first meeting out of Russia, away from all the gossipmongers. Natasha was to travel with her maid to Copenhagen from Chexbres, via Berlin. A week before their reunion she sent telegrams to Michael almost every day:

> I thank you so much my dear love you are always so good to me I kiss your dear hands with great tenderness I still

> cannot believe that I shall see you in a week these last days are going by so slowly. I am so unhappy living without you my Misha I write to you every day we are leaving the day after tomorrow for Berlin I kiss you with all my heart let me know how your health is at the moment. May God keep you – Natasha.
>
> I was so happy to receive your dear telegrams and fourth letter also to learn that you are well I hope you are not hiding anything from me I am also better I thank you my angel for your care. It seems to me that Sunday will never arrive I want to see you so much I kiss you tenderly and lovingly – Natasha.
>
> Received your telegram late yesterday night we leave one thirty five hope to have time to receive news before departure also evening Adlon I am happy to be leaving in order to be nearer you. Promise me to look after yourself stay indoors for a few days also do not hide anything from me I feel so sad and depressed without you I kiss you tenderly – Natasha.

Then finally she arrived in Berlin:

> Arrived Berlin eleven night going on soonest possible. If you have time wire me Adlon own name. Undecided what name to take in D. Am so happy – Natasha.

Then at last she arrived in Copenhagen and immediately sent a telegram to Michael at the Amalienborg Palace:

> Arrived Hotel d'Angleterre room 102 will await you all day impatiently – Natasha.

Michael hurried to the hotel and they were together again. But only twelve days later he had to return to Russia. Their leave-taking was even more terrible and painful this time, if that were possible. Michael bought a post card of the hotel showing a picture of the front of the building and wrote to Natasha:

> *Copenhagen 13th August 1909.*
> My darling, beautiful Natasha, there are not enough words with which I could thank you for all that you are giving me in my life. Our stay here will be always the brightest memory of my whole existence. Don't be sad – with God's help we shall meet again very soon. Please do always believe all my words and my tenderest love to thee, to my darling, dearest star, whom I will never, never leave or abandon. I embrace you and kiss you all over . . . . Please believe me that I am all yours, Misha.

Natasha returned to Chexbres, unhappy and lonely. It was not long before she decided to go back to Russia; both Michael and she were suffering from their enforced separation, and they felt that anything would be better than this. While Natasha was beginning to make her arrangements for the journey back to Russia, news arrived of Michael's ill-health. She cabled him:

> Am terribly worried unable to reserve seat. Telegraph me immediately what is the matter with you what is your temperature. If your illness is bad I will try leave tomorrow for Petersburg without stopping Berlin only must have your answer today my dear love answer me without hiding anything beg you. May God keep you. I kiss you tenderly – Natasha.

Michael must have managed to reassure her, for her next telegrams to him do not sound quite so frantically worried.

> Thanks for telegram I am in a hurry have bought ticket for tomorrow evening I hope your hand is better I am so upset and unhappy without you I kiss you with all my heart may God keep you – Natasha.
>
> We arrived here yesterday evening thanks two dear cables

the first one received before departure but too late to answer I am happy to know you are better I beg you to look after yourself. I am so impatient to see you again very quickly I love you so much my Misha I kiss you with infinite tenderness – Natasha.

As Natasha drew nearer and nearer to Russia she began to worry about the sort of reception she was going to find awaiting her at the frontier, and she sent Michael the following cable:

> Received telegram not reassured. *Enfin qui vivra verra.* Wire me to arrive 11 pm frontier Granica. Vienna train Wagon Lit number 17. I also rejoice – Natasha.

Again Michael must have managed to reassure her, for she wired him immediately:

> Thanks from heart for dear cables and letters I only think of leaving here to meet you very soon your dear letters have so comforted me I kiss your hands in gratitude and tenderness – Natasha.

Evidently there was no trouble at the frontier after all:

> Thanks dear telegram. Long to see you. Wire me to Minsk what time tomorrow you will be at Olga's I kiss you and love you with all my being.

So Natasha returned to Russia and to Michael.

4 Marriage

Natasha rented a small furnished house in Moscow near the Petrovisky Park, and as soon as she was settled, telegraphed to Chexbres to tell the governess who had stayed on there with Tata to come back to Moscow as soon as possible. Tata rejoined her mother and they passed the winter very quietly in their new home. Tata had lessons every day at home from the governess and learned all the usual subjects including French and English. Natasha stayed at home as much as was possible as she preterred to be away from all the gossip and sneers. Michael travelled from Gatchina to Moscow as often as he could. They were very happy that winter, and in spite of the difficult circumstances, laughter was frequently heard coming from that house during the long evenings. Michael was on leave for Christmas and they spent it together in the usual style with presents for everybody. It was a very gay and happy time for them all. A few weeks later Natasha realized that she was expecting a child. When she told Michael he wept with happiness, but after a while he started to become so frantic with worry for her, that she had to try to reassure him. There was nothing that they could do except await the birth of their child as peacefully as possible. He dared not defy his brother and marry Natasha; anyway he would need the Tsar's permission to wed before any Russian priest would dare to conduct such a marriage service. Natasha managed to remain the calmer of the two.

When spring arrived they rented a house in the country called Udinka, and it was surrounded by lovely woods and a pretty lake with a bathing-house. On Natasha's birthday Michael arranged for a magnificent display of fireworks in her honour, and decorated a special chair as a throne for her and covered it with field daisies. Unfortunately Natasha suffered from hay-fever, and these flowers set her off sneezing, but Michael insisted that she sit there, so she sneezed and sneezed and laughed the whole time. Some evenings Michael brought a chair into the garden for himself, and sat for hours beneath the trees playing his flute. But his pet poodle, Cuckoo, who obviously did not appreciate music for the flute, lifted up his head and howled until Michael, exasperated, chased him back into the house. Natasha laughed until she cried. Her own pet dog, a mongrel named Jack, seemed to accept flute-playing as completely normal and did not even twitch his ears very much as the sound of the instrument echoed around the garden. Jack was a sort of fox-terrier who had attached himself one day to Natasha and who, since then, hardly ever left her side. He was terribly ugly, but very intelligent and absolutely devoted to her.

At the beginning of August Natasha and Michael returned to Moscow to prepare for the birth of their son who arrived on the 6th of the month. Michael and a friend had left Natasha quietly resting and had gone for a walk; on their return they found Natasha in her bed with her son in her arms. They decided to call him

George, after Michael's brother who had died. After a few weeks they returned to Udinka with George, and in spite of everything they were so happy and proud of their little son. He was a fat placid infant with rosy cheeks and big blue eyes, and later on he grew a mass of golden curls.

It was not long before Natasha had completely recovered from the birth, and they resumed their gay and carefree lives. There were almost always friends visiting, and they would all go out on the usual drives, picnics and bathing parties. In the autumn they went hunting for mushrooms and Natasha would supervise the sorting-out of them at home. Russians love wild mushrooms and find them much more tasty to eat than cultivated kinds. Of course, the people who went picking these mushrooms in the woods and fields were experts and knew exactly which variety were poisonous and which were good to eat. Natasha was one of these, and she would supervise not only the picking of them, the sorting-out, but also their destinies. Some were set aside to be eaten that same day; others were put away for pickling in vinegar, and still others were dried to be used in cooking in the winter. To celebrate Natasha's and Tata's name-day on 26th August, there was a party and a display of fireworks. Afterwards the grown-ups played hide-and-seek among the lilac bushes like a lot of children, laughing and calling to each other. So the summer passed by, and when the autumn mists began to cover the lake, they returned to Moscow for the winter.

There was now an unpleasant fact to be faced; summer and its lighthearted laughter and games were now over, and there were problems to be owned up to –

they could not be put aside any longer. The fact was that Natasha was still Wulfert's wife. Therefore George was Wulfert's son, at least the Law said so. Michael was very upset about this; adoring his son as he did, he wanted to acknowledge him. Natasha consulted her brother-in-law in his capacity of solicitor to ask his advice. Matveiev was a very clever and astute man, and he undertook to negotiate with Wulfert; if the latter could be persuaded to renounce paternity of George in a document, then all would be well, and Michael would then be able to recognize his own son. But would Wulfert agree to take such a step? How could he be made to agree? After long and painfully drawn-out discussions and correspondence, Wulfert finally agreed to renounce his wife's son for the sum of 200,000 roubles (£20,000). And so it happened; George was acknowledged to be the son of the Grand Duke.

The next summer they decided to visit Brassowo which was a night's journey from Moscow. Michael had his private railway carriage which was hooked onto the ordinary train. There was no actual station at Brassowo, but the train stopped especially for them and a red carpet was laid down for them to walk on to reach the waiting carriages, and then they were driven the two miles to the house. Cars were not possible at Brassowo as the roads were just tracks and deep ruts made by carriage and cart wheels. The coachmen wore black waistcoats with brightly coloured sleeves, and in their round black hats they wore peacock feathers. The house was a big rambling wooden one with huge rooms and beautiful parquet floors. There was a lovely garden with a croquet lawn, swings, fountains and a swimming pool and stables, as well as the home farm. The estate was self-supporting except for certain items of groceries, and there was a bakery which made all the bread and cakes. There were hardly ever less than sixteen people for meals.

That summer there were the usual picnics. The major-domo would go off in advance with some servants to a pre-selected site and they would erect portable tables and chairs and then lay out all the food. There would be caviar, smoked salmon, cold sturgeon, and vegetable salads. If the weather were a bit chilly a bonfire was lit and they would cook sausages and baked potatoes, after which Michael and the other men present would amuse themselves by leaping over the embers.

When that summer ended, they returned to St Petersburg and rented an apartment. At long last Natasha's divorce was heard, and then was over. She was no longer Wulfert's wife. One day, when George was fourteen months old, Natasha left him and Tata in Nyanya's care, and Michael and she went to Bavaria for a short holiday. While they were staying in the village of Berchtesgaden, they secretly crossed the border into Austria and were married in the Serbian Church in Vienna. As both the Serbian and Russian Churches are Eastern Orthodox, there was nothing anyone could do about this marriage. It was a perfectly legal one in Russia and indeed everywhere else. But George remained a commoner, the child of a morganatic marriage.

Michael and Natasha sent a telegram to Nicholas to tell him of their marriage. On hearing the news, the Tsar was furious for many reasons; one of them was the shock of yet another marital scandal in his family, for this one came as the most recent of a whole train of them. Within a few years of Nicholas's succession to the throne, his cousin, Grand Duke Michael (one of the six sons of Grand Duke Michael senior, and the grandson of Nicholas I) had married a commoner in the very teeth of the Emperor's ban, and had settled in England, never to return again to Russia. Then the Tsar's uncle, Grand Duke Alexis fell in love with Princess Zina, wife of Prince Eugene of Leuchtenberg; there was no divorce in this case, and so the scandal was all the greater. Next Anastasia, Princess of Montenegro and Duchess of Leuchtenberg divorced her husband and married Grand Duke Nicholas, the Tsar's cousin; another uncle, left a widower, married a divorcée. Two and a half years after this his own first cousin, Grand Duke Cyril married Victoria-Melita, the divorced wife of the Grand Duke of Hesse; and now his own brother . . . it was unbearable. On top of all this, Nicholas had been beside himself with worry about the health of his son Alexis; it was becoming a real possibility that his son would never be strong enough to mount the throne of Imperial Russia, even if he lived long enough, which at times seemed doubtful. Now came the astounding news that the next in the line of succession after Alexis had married a commoner and a somewhat notorious woman. Nicholas complained to friends:

> He broke his word, his word of honour. How, in the midst of the boy's illness and all our troubles could they have done such a thing?

He wrote to his mother that this marriage of his brother's was to be kept a complete secret in the family only, but of course this was impossible. He was

MARRIAGE

eventually obliged to recognize it, and he granted Natasha the title of Countess Brassow. But to show his displeasure he banished them from Russia. It now seems clear that Michael must have realized that if he wanted Natasha as his wife he was going to have to act quickly. If the Tsarevich had suddenly died at that time, Michael would have become Heir Apparent, and it would have been impossible for him ever to marry Natasha.

As for Captain Wulfert, it was not long before he managed to console himself. He married one of the daughters of a rich Moscow merchant called Petukhov. In later years, when Natasha spoke of her young days, she never mentioned her marriage to Wulfert. She would just say that she had been married to Mamontoff when she was very young, and had given birth to her daughter. The whole story of her second marriage from start to finish had not been very honourable so she conveniently forgot all about it; it was as if Wulfert had never been.

5 Exile and Pardon

So Michael, Natasha, Tata and George plus several servants and a governess left Russia in 1912 and travelled for some time round Europe. Their first stop was at Cannes where they took over a whole floor at the Hotel du Parc. Once Chaliapin, who had a singing engagement at Monte Carlo, came to see them. Michael suddenly developed a passion for playing practical jokes; He loved to put hair brushes and damp sponges in people's beds, sew up their pyjama legs and fill them with confetti, set alarm clocks to ring at all sorts of odd hours, and once he covered one of Tata's dolls with glue and bristles cut from a clothes brush; the sight of her darling doll so disfigured caused the poor child to howl with fright. They would take motor trips to Grasse, to the Gorges du Loup and other places of interest along the coast. After Easter the weather began to be too hot, so they packed their things and left for Chexbres where they spent the summer. In late August they left for Bad Kissengen and from there they went to England where Michael had taken a lease of Knebworth House from Lord Lytton. But there was the problem of the dogs. Realising that England had strict quarantine laws regarding them, Michael had written to the King to ask what could be done about his dogs. The only concession that was made was that the dogs were allowed to be kept in the grounds at Knebworth in specially built kennels and runs for the requisite quarantine period. Knebworth remained their base but Michael and Natasha continued to travel quite a bit. They went to St Moritz after Christmas for winter sports, and they spent Easter at Cannes. They hated the publicity that their romance and marriage had engendered, and they tried to live quietly and see only close private friends. However, one evening in Monte Carlo, they allowed themselves to be persuaded to dine out at a restaurant for a change. They had been assured by their host that this particular restaurant was a very exclusive one, and that nothing could possibly happen to annoy them there. But it so happened that there was a certain English woman there that night who at the sight of Natasha and Michael forgot her manners and stared at them through her lorgnette during the entire meal. Natasha tried to pay no attention but suddenly could control her temper no longer. She snatched up a soup spoon from the table and raising it to her eye, pretended to stare through it at the English woman, who confused, returned to eating her meal. Although there was a great deal of laughter later at this incident, there was also an undercurrent of bitterness. It was just the kind of situation that they were trying to avoid.

But they were very happy living at Knebworth; they invited close friends to stay and enjoyed giving parties for them. Chaliapin came to see them, and once they entertained members of the Russian Ballet including the prima ballerina Karsavina. On the mornings after the parties, the gardeners were not allowed to start work in the part of the garden near the house, so as to leave undisturbed the slumbers of the guests who would eventually rise yawning just in time for lunch. Natasha took to the grand life at Knebworth and enjoyed giving orders to the many footmen who were always dressed in knee-breeches and white stockings. Sometimes Natasha and Michael went to the opera in London, and once or twice they went to the races. Michael took music lessons and learned to play the guitar and the mandolin. They kept horses and rode round the countryside very often, but Michael despised hunting; after having been after wolf and bear in Russia, he felt that to chase after a fox was rather tame and ignoble.

During the summer of 1913 they travelled again and re-visited Chexbres. For Natasha's twenty-fifth birthday Michael bought her a picture postcard showing a green grassy place with snowdrops growing among trees, and with distant snow-covered mountains. On the back he wrote:

> My dearest Natashechka, With all my heart I congratulate you, and from the depth of my soul wish you the best of health and happiness for a thousand years. I regret that there are very few articles suitable for presents here, but to them is added a Rolls-Royce that will be awaiting its mistress in Paris. Kissing you very tenderly, your Misha.

In September of that year they were in Paris. Michael decided to take an excursion to the top of the Eiffel Tower. Natasha refused to accompany him as she had no head for heights. Michael must have been feeling a little home-sick for Russia, for from the top of the Eiffel Tower he wrote Natasha a postcard and posted it in the special letter box there:

Gatchina is almost visible from this height. Kissing you tenderly, Your Misha.

In 1914 came the war and with it the Tsar's pardon. They immediately packed their belongings and put them in store, and taking with them only the bare necessities, they set off to return to Russia. They embarked at Liverpool on board *SS Venus*. The first night out was very rough and Natasha and Tata's governess were seasick. During the night the ship was joined by an escort of British destroyers. The governess, forgetting her sickness, got out of her bunk to cheer the British, as did everyone else except Natasha; she was feeling far too ill and remained in her bunk. However, she was heard to remark that the governess could not have been feeling all that ill if she were able to jump about cheering wildly in the middle of the night. This caused quite a lot of bad feeling between the two women. Eventually they arrived at Bergen, and from there travelled to Christiania (Oslo), Stockholm, and then through Finland to St Petersburg and Gatchina.

Michael re-joined the army and was sent to command the savage Caucasian Division at the front in Galicia.

For a present in the New Year Natasha gave Michael a diary, beautifully covered in blue leather with the Russian crown and his initials tooled in gold on the front cover, and he began to write entries each day. It became a habit which continued through the next years right up until March 1918 when he was suddenly called away one day. . . . The entries for 1915 give us a picture of their everyday lives. For instance, for the 3rd

January he wrote:

> At 10 a.m. the Wiasemskys, Johnson [Michael's secretary] and I went to detestable Petrograd. I went to my house on the embankment, where I have a hospital for 100 wounded soldiers and 25 officers and where Shleifer is in charge. Then I went to see Mamma at the Anichkov Palace and stayed until 3 p.m. After that I went with Natasha to do some shopping until 4 p.m. and then I went to Tsarskoe Selo to see Nicky. Then after visiting the Shleifers, I returned to Gatchina. Weather was overcast with 3° of frost.

Michael had his private railway coach attached to the staff train near the front, and Natasha was able to spend time with him, staying in the coach. Whenever they could be together, they were, even if it meant a lot of travelling. Michael wrote in his diary on 12th February 1915:

> At 6.30 a.m. Girard, Koka [Michael's ADC] and I drove in the car to Lvov where we arrived after 2 hours drive. Natasha arrived here in the afternoon. We had dinner and went to bed late. The weather was dull and it was freezing in the evening. What a tremendous joy to be with my beloved Natashechka again!

One of the entries in Michael's diary was written by Natasha herself:

> 10th March 1915, Lvov. My dear Mishechka, I am so terribly sad to part with you. When you return from the station and read these lines you will know that my thoughts will always be with you, that I love you dearly and will miss you terribly. Embracing you tenderly, may God bless and keep you, your Natasha.

Then troubles arrived for Natasha; first of all her sister Olga died suddenly in Moscow. Natasha went there for the funeral and stayed for a week. Then, soon afterwards Michael got diphtheria and was quite ill for a while but soon recovered. Then Vera, her other sister became ill and died, and Natasha was in Moscow once again for a funeral and to be with her mother. When she returned to Gatchina Michael was still at home convalescing from his illness.

It must have been around this time that Maurice Paléologue, the French Ambassador to Russia, came across Natasha in a shop in St Petersburg. With a Frenchman's delight and appreciation of a beautiful woman he wrote later:

> I saw a slender young woman of about thirty. She was a delight to watch. Her whole style revealed great personal charm and refined taste. Her chinchilla coat, opened at the neck gave a glimpse of a dress of silver grey taffeta with trimmings of lace. Her pure and aristocratic face is charmingly modelled and she has light velvety eyes. Around her neck a string of superb pearls sparkled in the light. There was a dignified, sinuous, soft gracefulness about her every movement.

One day, just as Natasha was about to get into her car after a shopping trip in St Petersburg, she caught sight of a man walking towards her on the pavement; there was something about this man that looked familiar to her, and then, as he came closer, she suddenly recognized him as her old friend, Dimitri Abrikossow, who had been one of her first admirers when she was a young girl in Moscow. She greeted him with joy, and after chatting with him for a while, she invited him to lunch with Michael and herself at Gatchina the following Sunday. Abrikossow was nervous at the idea of meeting the Grand Duke, and Natasha laughed at him. She told him to think of Michael just as her husband,

and to forget that he was the brother of the Emperor. Abrikossow said that he would. He wrote later in his *Memoirs*:

> When I duly arrived at her house, the first person I met was the Grand Duke, and was immediately captivated by his charm. Eventually we became good friends, and I must say I have never met another man so uncorrupted and noble in nature; it was enough to look into his clear blue eyes to be ashamed of any bad thought or insincere feeling. In many ways he was a grown-up child who had been taught only what was good and moral. He did not want to admit that there was wickedness and falsehood in this world and trusted everybody. Had his wife not watched over him constantly, he would have been deceived at every step.

Abrikossow teased Natasha and admitted to her that he had been gently in love with her a long time ago, and that when he had heard of her marriage to Michael, he had been extremely sceptical of the outcome of such a union. However, now that he had met her husband, he had found him to be infinitely superior in character to his wife. . . .

Abrikossow spent nearly all his Sundays at Gatchina, and there met other members of the Romanoff family. He would listen to their talks and discussions:

> The first impression I had was that the Romanoffs had ideas that were centuries old, and that they did not know how the rest of Russia lived and did not want to learn. Fundamentally they felt that Russia existed for the Romanoffs, not the Romanoffs for Russia.

He was very interested in Natasha, and to see how she had grown up, and into what sort of person the schoolgirl that he had known had become:

> Nathalia Sergeievna had acquired a certain amount of regal manners – a vacant look, an artificial smile, elegance – but her mentality remained that of an independent girl who could not hide her feelings. I was present at some awkward scenes. At a luncheon attended by three Grand Dukes, for instance, she reacted to the news of another disaster on the front with the exclamation: 'It was you Romanoffs who brought Russia to such a state!' There was a general hush in the room and the Grand Dukes looked down at their plates. As I told Natasha afterwards, it was no wonder she was regarded at Court as a revolutionary.
>
> But her old liberalism did not prevent her from enjoying her new position. She was always elegantly dressed and wore magnificent jewellery; she enjoyed attracting the attention of the whole theatre as she appeared in her box at the ballet. She always invited me, and sitting somewhere behind her, I could not help taking pride in the gorgeous creature into which the modest schoolgirl I had once adored had been transformed.

There are two entries in Michael's diary during this period which are of more than usual interest:

> 18th October 1915. At 6.15 Natasha, Anna A., Shilov and I drove to town. We dined and then went to the ballet. I sat with Boris*, and in the intervals we visited Natasha's box.

> 24th October. Petrograd. After dinner Natasha, the Shleifers and I went to the Mikhailov Theatre. Boris and I sat in the Imperial Box. . . .

So it would seem that even now, as a properly married woman, Natasha was not allowed to sit in the Imperial box with her husband. No wonder that she had acquired a certain amount of regal manners and that

---

* Grand Duke Boris Vladimirovitch.

she enjoyed attracting the attention of the whole theatre. . . It was a kind of self-defence for her so that no one would know how hurt she was by this. Michael went quite often to see his mother at her palace, and frequently went to Tsarskoe Selo to see Nicholas, but Natasha was never included in these visits. Michael would accompany her to friends' houses where he would rejoin her after having paid his visits to his mother and to his brother.

Olga saw her 'dear, darling Floppy' for a short time during this period. At that time she was working as a nurse with the Red Cross at Rovno, not far from the Polish-Austrian frontier. At the end of 1916 Michael arrived for a few days from the north. She did not have much spare time but she managed to give him every moment that she could. They did not talk about the terrible times that they were living in, but rather remembered their happy childhood days, and they laughed together over amusing memories. But when the time came for Michael to leave, and Olga accompanied him to see him off at the station, they wept together unashamedly. They never saw each other again.

Nicholas may have welcomed Michael's visits to Tsarskoe Selo, and the Empress Marie may have been pleased to see her 'little Misha' back in Russia again, but some members of the Romanoffs refused to forgive him for what they considered his disastrous marriage. Natasha was disliked by them all and even feared, as she was known to be an extremely ambitious woman, and they would have nothing at all to do with her.

PART TWO
THE TIMES

6 Unrest and War

When the war had been declared in 1914 it had come as a welcome distraction to the Tsar and his Ministers from all the unrest and political stirrings that had been beginning to make themselves felt. Discontent had been rife among the people for many years. As far back as the reign of Nicholas I (1825–1855) the chief social question in Russia had been that of serfdom. Alexander II, his son and successor, had passed a law freeing the serfs and obliging the landlords to grant each peasant a plot of land for a fixed rent. As he said in a speech to the Moscow gentry:

> The present position cannot last and it is better to abolish serfdom from above than wait until it begins to be abolished from below.

But he remained unpopular, especially among the intellectuals, who felt that his reforms, such as they were, did not begin to touch the problems. In 1866 a student tried to assassinate him, but failed. Secret societies were formed which issued proclamations, but nothing came of this revolutionary wave as the organizers were quickly either executed or banished to Siberia. In 1879 a man fired five shots at the Tsar and missed; in 1880 a workman blew up the Imperial dining room at the

Winter Palace, but the Tsar was not there. Nevertheless he began to feel real fear and decided to sign an agreement to study the possibility of making some administrative and financial reforms, and agreed to appoint two committees for this purpose. On the very day that he signed this agreement, he was assassinated.

His son Alexander III was a very young man when he became Tsar, and the biggest influence in his life was his tutor, a man called Pobedonestsev. This man felt that the Tsar should be an Autocrat, and he drew up a manifesto which he gave to the Tsar to read out, and which proclaimed that he (Alexander) was 'chosen to defend' autocratic power. The molten lava in the revolutionary crater began to seethe and bubble as the Press was censored, Jews persecuted, and all revolutionary organizations destroyed. Matters were not helped by the arrival of a famine in 1891; the subsequent shortages of almost every commodity produced more unrest. This time the unrest was not only felt in the fields but also among the workers in the ever-increasing number of factories. For Russia had by now become an industrial country, and it was in the factories that Socialism turned into Marxism.

The Grand Duchess Olga, looking back at those times and commenting on them in her memoirs writes:

> ... my father was considered a reactionary – and I suppose he was – in a sense. But consider the circumstances in which he came to the throne. What choice had he but to suppress the terrorists? He was opposed to irresponsible liberalism and he refused to placate people who wanted to introduce the governmental forms of Great Britain and France. Remember – our intellectuals were a minority. The majority of the people, what could they have made of

a democratic government? My grandfather had started many reforms. I know that my father was deeply concerned about improvements in education and the standard of living – but a mere thirteen years was not enough – especially when you remember the conditions at the beginning of the reign. And he died at forty-nine! . . .

After the death of his father in 1894 Nicholas inherited an extremely complicated situation and was incapable of coping with it. One of Alexander III's greatest mistakes during his life was to ignore the fact that Nicholas was his heir and would one day be Tsar. Statesmanship had played no part in the education of the young Nicholas, and only in 1893 when he was 25, for the very first time was Nicholas invited to sit on a Council of State. It was as if Alexander could not bear the idea of matters of state encroaching on their simple and innocent family life, and Nicholas was trained only as a soldier. When his father died and Nicholas became Tsar, he was terrified. Olga wrote later:

> Nicky was in despair. He kept saying that he did not know what would become of us all, that he was unfit to reign . . . It was my father's fault . . . And what a ghastly price was later paid for the mistake. Of course, my father, who had always enjoyed an athlete's health, could not have foreseen such an early end to his life . . . but the mistake was there.

During the first year of his reign, a deputation had come to Nicholas to beg him to carry out certain reforms and were answered as follows:

> . . . Let all know that I intend to defend the principle of autocracy as unswervingly as did my father.

The next day there appeared in a newspaper an 'Open

Letter' to the Tsar:

> Senseless dreams concerning yourself are no longer possible. If autocracy proclaims itself identical with the omnipotence of bureaucracy, its cause is lost . . . it digs its own grave . . . you first began the struggle, and the struggle will come . . .

In June of the following year, St Petersburg had its first strike of 30,000 workmen, but it seems that Nicholas paid no attention and thought it unimportant.

It was only a few years earlier that an external law student at St Petersburg University had obtained his degree. His name was Vladimir Ilyitch Ulyanov and he had studied Marxism and had become quite an authority on the subject.

Vladimir Ilyitch Ulyanov, later known as Lenin, was born in 1870 in a small town in the Middle Volga region called Simbirsk. By one of those strange coincidences that happen occasionally in history, Simbirsk was also the birthplace of another revolutionary, though of a different kind: Alexander Kerensky. In fact it was Kerensky senior, Feodor, who was the headmaster of the school which the young Vladimir Ilyitch Ulyanov attended, and it was Feodor Kerensky who wrote a glowing testimonial on the occasion of the young Vladimir's graduation from the school with the highest marks of his class. Vladimir was the third of six children; an older brother, Alexander, was arrested in 1887 in St Petersburg on a charge of attempting to assassinate Tsar Alexander III; in May of that year he was hanged. Vladimir, or Volodya as he was called in the family, started to attend the University of Kazan, but was very soon expelled for taking part in some minor student demonstrations. He then tried his hand at farming, at his mother's instigation, as she was terrified that her Volodya would get mixed up with politics and would go the same way as her Alexander. But Vladimir hated farming. He began to study law at home, and crammed four years hard work into one. At the same time he was reading, reading – any books that he could get; Pushkin, Turgenev, Dostoyevsky, Tolstoy and Karl Marx. When he took his law examinations he passed with the highest possible marks. At the same time that Nicholas was stating his unswerving devotion to autocracy, Vladimir Ilyitch Ulyanov left Russia for Geneva to establish contact with a group of exiled Russian and foreign Marxists in order to learn something about Socialism in Europe.

When Lenin returned from his travels in Europe, his activities caused him to be arrested for organizing strikes and for printing anti-government pamphlets, and he was sent to prison in St Petersburg for one year; he was then exiled to Siberia for a term of three years. He took with him to Siberia one thousand roubles and one hundred books, and he spent his time in studying, in corresponding with Marxists all over the world, and in writing a book called *The Development of Capitalism in Russia*. A woman, a fellow Marxist whom he had met in St Petersburg called Nadezda Krupskaya also arrived, exiled too to the same town. She eventually became Lenin's wife.

When at last the three years of exile were up, Lenin left for Munich, and then for London where he held meetings and helped to form a political party which they called the Russian Social Democratic Workers Party. In 1903, in Brussels, during the second conference of the R.S.D.W.P. it became obvious that some members did not agree with Lenin and his followers on various questions of policy. When the matter was put to the vote, Lenin and his group obtained the majority vote, (Bolshevik = of the majority); the others became known as Mensheviks (of the minority), and there was a rift within the Party.

Back in Russia the troubles and unrest continued. In 1904 Pleve, the Minister for Home Affairs, was killed when the carriage in which he was riding was blown up by a bomb. Nicholas wavered for more than a month before appointing a successor; the Russo-Japanese War was taking up all his attention. It was in 1903 that a Russian private company called the Yalu Timber Company had begun moving Russian soldiers into Korea disguised as ordinary workmen with the object of acquiring Korea as a new province of Russia. Nicholas had approved this plan, though there were those who thought it far too dangerous. Manchuria had been 'temporarily' occupied by Russia in order to finish the building of the Trans-Siberian railway; Port Arthur had been leased for ninety-nine years to the Russians by the Chinese; now the occupation of Korea made war with Japan absolutely inevitable. Pleve had remarked that he thought that a 'small victorious war' would be good for Russia and would serve to distract the people from the unrest at home. But Nicholas himself was unwilling actually to declare war on Japan; he was hoping for a peaceful settlement, and firmly believed that if he did not declare war, then it would not come. But in February 1904 Nicholas was horrified to receive a telegram informing him that Japanese destroyers had made a sudden attack on the Russian squadron anchored in the harbour at Port Arthur – without any previous warning or declaration of hostilities.

The war was a catastrophe; no one in Russia had realized that Japan had, in comparatively few years, progressed from a feudal nation into a strong modern industrial and military power. On land the Russian forces were overcome; at sea the Russian Eastern Fleet was almost completely crippled. Nicholas ordered the Russian Baltic Fleet to sail half-way round the world to restore Russian naval supremacy in the Pacific. So, under Admiral Rozhdestvenski, they set sail and began their long voyage to Japan. In the North Sea they mistook a British trawler for a German destroyer, and fired on her and sank her. After rounding the Cape of Good Hope they stopped at Madagascar for bunkers. The officers and crew were by this time in a very bad way; the conditions below decks in that terrible equitorial heat had made everyone sick; no one had experienced such heat before. Morale was very bad. They were obliged to wait at Madagascar for months for colliers and food supplies to arrive. At last they set sail for the Sea of Japan, and after a terrible passage, they engaged the Japanese in battle in the Straits of Tsushima. The whole Russian fleet was sunk.

After the news of this catastrophe reached Russia, Nicholas realized that there was no longer any chance of winning the war, and he sent the brilliant President of the Council of Ministers and former minister of finance, Count Witte, to America to negotiate peace terms. The treaty that was eventually signed was a dazzling compromise which saved Russia from ignominy, and it was entirely due to Witte's inspired diplomacy. However, the humiliation was there; Russia agreed, among other things, to surrender her lease of Port Arthur, evacuate Manchuria, and recognize Japan's sphere of influence in Korea. The treaty, which was signed in September 1905, brought even more unpopularity to the government.

Meanwhile, at home in 1904, a group of county councillors had met together and had prepared a petition which they presented to Nicholas. It called for inviolability of the person, freedom of conscience, of speech, of meeting, of the press, of association and equal civil rights. Nicholas uttered general promises but would say nothing definite. The chance of a peaceful compromise was passing by. In January 1905 thousands of working men led by a priest and singing hymns marched to the Winter Palace to speak to 'their' Tsar. Nicholas was away. The guards were confused at the sudden approach of the crowd and opened fire. About ninety-two people were killed and at least three hundred injured. At the beginning of February Grand Duke Sergius was blown up by a bomb at the Kremlin by a social revolutionary. Grand Duke Sergius was the husband of Alexandra's sister. In London that same year Lenin organized the third Congress of the Bolshevik R.S.D.W.P. and resolutions were passed promising support for the peasantry, confiscation of the large estates of the gentry, among other things. In Russia a deputation to Nicholas, repeating demands for inviolability of the person, was answered by the Tsar himself – 'The Tsar's will is unshakeable' Nicholas announced, but as a compromise he agreed to the formation of a council (Duma) formed of forty-three per cent peasants, thirty-four per cent landed proprietors, and twenty-three per cent county councillors. They were to discuss and draft new laws, but this did not put a stop to an ever-increasing number of strikes by the workers. These strikes culminated in October 1905 in a General Strike all over Russia. Nicholas told his Ministers that he was thinking of abdicating, but Count Witte, by now the Premier, managed to prevail upon the Tsar to sign a manifesto instead; this promised all the things that the deputation had asked for, *i.e.*, inviolability of the person, etc. . . . But the manifesto pleased no one. The right wing felt that Witte and the Tsar had gone too far, and the progressives felt that they had not gone nearly far enough.

At about this time a council of workmen's delegates (a Soviet), led by Trotsky and backed by Lenin, started publishing decrees and tried to play the part of a second government; on 3rd December all the members were arrested and this led to much shooting in the streets; armed guards were called out to put down the rioting. In April 1906 the first Duma convened and in its address to the throne proposed its own programme of law reforms. The Tsar replied that he could not accept the Duma's proposals, and so the first Duma dissolved itself. This set the pattern which lasted until 1917; Duma followed Duma; each one made its own proposals to the Tsar and stated its programme; each time Nicholas turned them down.

This was the state of affairs in 1914 when war was declared against Germany. Suddenly Nicholas was popular.

A burst of patriotic enthusiasm shook the whole country to

its very foundation. All other considerations were put aside, political strife forgotten. The strikes on which the Germans based such hopes, and which had cost them much, stopped at once, and the strikers became the warmest partisans of the coming war.*

There were endless patriotic demonstrations and processions marching through the streets of St Petersburg which was now to be known as Petrograd. Cheering crowds gathered in front of the British and French Embassies. Thousands of students, and older men as well, carried flags and portraits of Nicholas and of Alexis. They marched along singing the national anthem and other patriotic songs and hymns and made their way to the Winter Palace. There at the foot of the Alexander Column they all fell onto their knees singing *Boje Tsaria Khrani*! (God save the Tsar.) The anonymous author of *Russian Court Memoirs* continues:

> ... Never during the twenty years of his reign had the Emperor been so beloved, so respected, so popular in the eyes of his subjects as at this moment ... the veneration was so deep that men lifted their hats, and women – even well-dressed elegant ladies – made the sign of the cross ... the exaltation rose to such a pitch that it seemed as if an electric touch had united the Tsar and his people and made them one in heart and feeling ....

But this 'burst of patriotic enthusiasm' did not last for very long, and the news of serious retreats by the army from Poland and Galicia turned it into a wave of pessimism. The fourth Duma proposed to the Tsar the formation of a National Coalition Government 'possessing the confidence of the country', but Nicholas could not accept the inclusion of the Liberal ministers.

* *Russian Court Memoirs*, published in England by Herbert Jenkins in 1917.

The last chance of a peaceful solution and compromise was lost for ever, and in spite of the war, revolution was being seriously considered.

In view of the humiliating defeats suffered in the field, Nicholas felt that he should make himself Commander-in-Chief of the army in the place of his uncle, the Grand Duke Nicholas. The Tsar wrote a beautifully composed letter to his uncle, thanking him for the conscientious way in which he had carried out his duties, but pointing out that the recent military defeats proved that all was not well, and that as he, the Tsar, was responsible to his people for the conduct of the war, that he therefore considered it to be his duty to take over the command. Thus it was, that at this crucial time in the political life of his country, that Nicholas was away at headquarters most of the time, and had left his wife Alexandra to deal with the problems of state at home.

The Empress had never been popular; now, at this time especially, she was mistrusted by everyone – mainly because of her German origin. Comparisons were made with the Queen of the Belgians, who by birth was also German, but who seemed to be greatly loved by her subjects. But Alexandra continued to be reproached by hers. The author of *Russian Court Memoirs* had these comments to make about her:

> ... If Her Majesty had been more accessible to the public during these twenty-two years of her life in Russia, less enigmatical in her attitude and more natural in her bearing towards people, these doubts would never have arisen at the present crisis.... When Her Majesty visited Tver a few months ago, intent on inspecting the local war hospitals, her carriage was followed by the crowd's murmur of *'Niemka Iedet, niemka iedet'*. (There goes the

German.) History repeats itself, and one is reminded of the old French cry: 'l'Autrichienne' which followed the unfortunate Marie Antoinette.

By this time Alexandra had come to rely on the advice of Rasputin, first for his seemingly successful treatment of her haemophilic son, and later for what she thought were his wise and holy opinions of matters appertaining to problems of state.

7 Rasputin

Gregory Efimovitch Rasputin was born in 1871 in the village of Prokovskoe in the province of Tobolsk, in the heart of Siberia. In 1904 he left his wife and family and devoted himself to religion. He told them that he was directly inspired by God. He adopted the teachings of a sect who called themselves *Khlystys* who believed that salvation could only be achieved by repentance. Therefore the more one sinned, and the more evil one's deeds, then the deeper and more poignant would be one's repentance, and so the more likely it would be that one would be pardoned and obtain perfect forgiveness. He preached that only through him could the sinner be saved; that the sinner had to unite himself to Rasputin in soul and body and as he (Rasputin) was the source of light, then their sins would be destroyed.

The story of Rasputin has been told many times so that almost everyone knows about this extraordinary man who eventually became all-powerful, the uncrowned Tsar of Russia, and about his gargantuan appetite for women, food and drink. One of the great mysteries of those times is how such a man managed to become a favourite of Alexandra, who, from all accounts, was a fastidious, somewhat prim woman. It is said that Rasputin hardly ever washed; hardly ever combed his matted hair or his beard. It is said that he stank like a goat. Once again I quote from the account of my old friend, the anonymous author of *Russian Court Memoirs* who had the following to say about Rasputin (as this passage was written in 1916, Rasputin was then still alive . . .):

> Until quite lately the influence of Her Majesty's elder sister, the Grand Duchess Elisabeth Feodorovna was paramount at the Imperial Court. Inclined to mysticism, she encouraged the same tendency in her sister's mind. Occult science absorbed the Empress for several years and enhanced the original morbidness of her disposition. . . . It was she who introduced all kinds of priests, monks and *startsi* to Court circles. People in the western countries do not have the least notion of what a Russian *staretz* is. It is a man, generally a simple peasant, who having attained middle age, endeavours to give himself a venerable aspect by growing his hair and beard in flowing manes. Such men make wandering their calling, making continual pilgrimages from one monastery to another, sometimes extending their journeys to Mount Athos and the Holy Land. Provided with a staff and a knapsack, they tramp all over the country, finding shelter and food in the different convents they visit. . . . The peasantry look upon such *startsi* as men devoted to saintliness and asceticism; even the merchant classes . . . have a great predilection for these wanderers. They invite them to their houses, ply them with food and countless glasses of fragrant tea and listen open-mouthed to their stories about their wandering life, their adventures and the miracles they have witnessed at different sacred shrines. . . . This calling leaves a wide range of possibilities to the idle and ne'er-do-wells who prefer a roving life to honest labour. . . . It seems preposterous to imagine such an uncouth individual amongst courtiers close to the steps of one of the most powerful thrones, wielding an influence on the developments of State events. . . .

And this author goes on to comment on the fact that Rasputin had managed to convince the Empress that her son's welfare depended on his (Rasputin's) presence, and that every time that Rasputin was sent away to Siberia somewhere, then each time something happened to the boy's health. This all strengthened Alexandra's superstitious belief in Rasputin's power, and his influence grew and grew. He did not content himself with his social successes, which from all accounts were considerable; women, it is said, fought for the privilege of sharing his bed, odiferous as he was. But he also started to interfere in the political and state problems of the day and took it upon himself to advise Alexandra as to how she should deal with them. Several of the Grand Dukes, among them the Tsar's brother, were extremely worried at the whole situation, and delegated Grand Duke Nicholas Mikhailovitch to write to the Tsar at headquarters:

> ... are you properly informed about the situation? ... Do you know the whole truth, or do they hide most of it from you? Where does the root of the evil lie? Let me explain in a few words; so long as your method of choosing your ministers was only known to a small *côterie*, things could carry on for better or worse. But as soon as such matters were generally known and discussed in public, it became obvious that Russia could not go on being governed in that way. You often told me that you trusted no one and were constantly being betrayed. If it is true, the remark should apply above all to your wife, who, though she loves you, is constantly leading you into error – surrounded as she is by people in the grip of the spirit of evil. You believe in Alexandra Feodorovna. That is natural. But the words she utters are the outcome of clever intrigues, they are not the truth. If you are powerless to

rid yourself of such influences, at least be always on your guard against the unceasing and systematic intriguers who use your wife as a tool. . .

Everyone was talking about the Empress and Rasputin, and her friendship with him was causing an enormous scandal. It was even rumoured that he was the father of the poor Tsarevitch Alexis, although the instigators of that particular rumour did not bother to note that Alexis, who was born in 1904, was therefore conceived before Rasputin had first arrived at St Petersburg. Alexandra complained about the everlasting gossip, but did not seem to realize that it was partly her fault. She could have put an end to it by removing Rasputin from her circle of intimate friends, but this she refused to do. She did not wish to risk the health of her beloved son and she believed that Rasputin's presence was necessary to protect him from his illness.

In December 1916 Rasputin was murdered, and in the morning his dead body was found beneath the ice on the river. The story of the evening of his death and of his murder has been the subject of plays, films and books, and it is one of the most horrific and dramatic happenings of pre-revolutionary Russia. That evening Rasputin had been invited by the young Prince Felix Youssoupoff to his palace for an evening's entertainment and music in the company of other friends, among them Grand Duke Dimitri. Some *petits fours* had been previously injected with arsenic, and Rasputin, who had a sweet tooth, consumed a large quantity. But it seems that the very sweetness of the cakes must have acted as an antidote to the poison; at any rate Rasputin suffered not at all from them. Youssoupoff and Dimitri were horrified and began to panic. Youssoupoff took up a revolver and shot Rasputin three times through the body. Still he stayed on his feet, though by now he was blaspheming in a terrible fashion and threatening them with punishment. A servant took up a knife and stabbed Rasputin in the back. At last he fell to the floor though he did not die. They bound and gagged him and carried him down to the river which was completely frozen over. A hole was made in the ice, and they threw him in. Incredibly, Rasputin managed to free himself from his bonds, and tried to clamber out from the hole in the ice, and he very nearly succeeded. They forced him back and held his head under the water. Then, and only then, did Rasputin die, and his body was carried away by the current under the ice.

Some time before this, Rasputin had had a premonition of his impending death, and he had written a letter which was found in his rooms after his murder. He announced that, if he were murdered at the hands of members of the House of Romanoff, then that would presage the end of Imperial Russia:

> . . . I feel that I shall leave life before January 1. I wish to make known to the Russian people, to Papa, to the Russian Mother and to the children, to the land of Russia, what they must understand. If I am killed by common assassins, especially by my brothers the Russian peasants, you, Tsar of Russia, have nothing to fear; remain on your throne and govern, and you, Russian Tsar, will have nothing to fear for your children, they will reign for hundreds of years in Russia. But if I am murdered by *boyars*, nobles, and if they shed my blood, their hands will remain soiled with my blood, for twenty-five years they will not wash their hands of my blood. They will leave Russia. Brothers will kill brothers, and they will kill each other

and hate each other, and for twenty-five years there will be no nobles in the country. Tsar of the land of Russia, if you hear the sound of the bell which will tell you that Gregory has been killed, you must know this: if it was your relations who have wrought my death then no one of your family, that is to say, none of your children or relations will remain alive for more than two years. They will be killed by the Russian people. . . . I shall be killed. I am no longer among the living. Pray, pray, be strong, think of your blessed family.

Gregory.

The blow of Rasputin's murder did not change Alexandra from her course, and she refused to face the fact that the country was on the point of revolution. She continued to insist that no important matters be decided without her, and anyone who dared to criticize her was either exiled to their country estates or sent to Siberia. She felt that she was at war with everybody, and that it was absolutely necessary for her to be firm. In January 1917 she said to the Grand Duchess Victoria, the wife of the Grand Duke Cyril, 'I have been on the throne for twenty-two years. I know Russia. I know how the people love our family. Who would dare to side against us?'

On 11th March 1917 the Duma was adjourned. The next day was the first day of the revolution.

8 Revolution and Abdication

The revolution took place in two phases – the March Revolution and the October Revolution. The first was caused by dissatisfaction on the part of the democratic elements with the conduct of the war; the second exploited the war weariness in the interests of the revolutionary doctrines of Marxism. It was the March Revolution which overthrew the Romanoffs, and the October one which re-built Russia. General Krymov wanted to seize the Tsar in his train and compel him to abdicate in favour of the Tsarevitch with the Grand Duke Michael as regent, at the same time arrest the Tsar's ministers, and then announce the abdication and the formation of a new government simultaneously. But the strikes and unrest meant postponement of this plan, and the advent of the March Revolution made it unnecessary. The strikes on the first day involved at least one hundred and thirty thousand working men demanding higher wages at the factories. The Duma, the government and the police paid little attention except in taking the necessary measures to prevent the strikers from reaching the centre of Petrograd. The second day more workers demonstrated, about thirty per cent of all Petrograd workers, and the mood changed and became sinister and threatening, and by now the university students had joined in as well. The third day the strike became general. The strikers were by now extremely aggressive and raided police stations, disarming the entire force. The Tsar telegraphed the Military Governor of Petrograd, General Khabaloff, ordering the strike to be suppressed. At first, the military's efforts at suppression were successful, but then the regiments themselves began to mutiny. The Duma wanted a new government to be formed immediately, and Rodzyanko, the Speaker, sent a telegram to the Tsar begging him to act quickly, which ended: '.... may the blame not fall on the wearer of the crown....' Nicholas paid no attention. Maurice Paléologue wrote of the Tsar in his diary at the time:

> Everything he said, and especially the long intervals of silence, his vague, unseeing eyes, his wandering thoughts, his strange over-wrought appearance — all these confirmed the idea in circulation for some months, that the Tsar already felt he was being swept away by destiny, had already lost all faith in his mission or in anything he did, had abdicated in spirit, resigned himself to imminent catastrophe, and was awaiting martyrdom.

Some regiments were ordered to return from parts of the front, their job being to protect the monarchy and keep order. But when the troops arrived at the railway stations, they found that pickets were awaiting them in order to stop them from getting through to the palace. By the time that this situation was sorted out, the impetus of the revolution was too strong to be stopped by armed forces. On the 25th March, Petrograd was in the hands of the mutinous regiments and the mob. Kerensky took charge of the security of the Duma and sent a message to the Tsar asking him to appoint a new

Prime Minister. Nicholas failed to reply at all. Two days later, despite the Tsar's continuing silence, they made up their minds to form a new government; their aim was to try to deal with the increasing anarchy and save the monarchy and the dynasty. While the Duma was electing this new government, workers had formed a Soviet themselves. This Soviet consisted of two hundred and fifty men – Socialist Duma deputies, workers, workers' leaders, and members of various strike committees. They appointed a strong executive committee which took over the distribution of food supplies and the defence of the city against any possible attacks by the autocracy. This Soviet became the real power, but nevertheless it worked with and upheld the decisions of the Duma. However, it was composed primarily of Mensheviks who believed that the revolution was to establish a democracy and not a dictatorship; and when Lenin arrived in Petrograd three weeks later, his main problem was to inspire his own party with enthusiasm for deepening the revolution, the Bolsheviks being in a definite minority in the Petrograd Soviet.

The Grand Duke Nicholas Mikhailovitch, an uncle of Michael's, was in Petrograd at that time. He had some very good French friends in Paris named Masson, and during this period he wrote to them almost every day detailing the happenings and adding his comments.* In a letter to the Massons dated 6/9 April 1917 he wrote as follows:

> It is a strange thing, but the whole of Russia is peaceful, especially in the countryside. The peasants continue working their fields without paying the slightest attention

* Grand Duke Nicholas Mikailovitch. *La Fin du Tsarisme, lettres inédites à Frederic Masson (1914–1918)*, Payot, Paris. 1968.

to the *coup d'état* which has changed everything in the space of forty eight hours. But in the towns, at the railway stations and main cross roads are meetings and conferences of all kinds, led by workers or soldiers; for the latter have deserted their regiments *en masse*, both regiments at the front and also behind the line. There are those soldiers who are on regular leave but they are in the minority. The rest move around and travel from one town to another without paying a penny in fares. . . . As to order in the towns and on the roads, it is excellent and in much better order than in the days of the old police. The real trouble-spots are the stations where there are soldiers all over the place with no one in command, taking over carriages by force and expelling the passengers. . . .

The Duma went ahead and formed a Provisional Government, even though no word had come from the Tsar. Prince Lvov was made Prime Minister, Milyukov Minister for Foreign Affairs, Tereshchenko Finance Minister, Guchkov Minister for War, and Kerensky Minister of Justice.

The Grand Duke Nicholas Mikhailovitch wrote to his friend in Paris:

Petrograd 14/27 April 1917.
Anarchy and order reign here in Petrograd, even though this sounds like a contradiction in terms. Thus, in spite of the absence of the usual police who have been replaced by beardless youths who now form the new military police, the traffic flows more freely than before. I have never seen so many pedestrians in the Nevsky Prospekt, in the Great Morskaia, on the quays or in the squares; and everyone seems to be laughing, confident and enjoying life and so-called 'liberty'. As for 'fraternity' it is relative. And as for the famous 'equality', it does not exist, and it is from this that anarchy springs. The soldiers from the garrison, as well as those from the outside, and deserters in military uniform take over everything, enter everywhere, give

orders, shout, hold meetings, but on the whole remain good tempered and do not kill anyone. There were more than one hundred thousand of this kind of soldier here, but gradually their numbers decrease as the rougher ones are sent to the front. (Small consolation for those who are already there!). . . . Kerensky, Tereshchenko, Nekrassoff form the left wing of the cabinet, but being the minority they are obliged to suffer the feebleness of the leaders – Prince Lvov and his followers, *e.g.* men like the illustrious Milyukov, Guchkov, etc., etc. Prince Lvov is the sort of idealist, a straight-forward man at all times, that your revolution produced in some *Girondins*. He will risk nothing, never lose his temper, and would rather let himself be killed than show any aggression. Kerensky is another type altogether. He is a totally convinced Socialist, but is a fine man with a will of iron. If one day he becomes President of the Council, he will never hesitate to use force to gain his ends, and especially to maintain order. Even as Minister of Justice he is everywhere where there is danger. It is he who speaks out, who acts, who gives orders and takes total responsibility. He is the go-between for the Provisional Government and the Soldiers and Workers Committees. With him gone, the Cabinet would inevitably topple – that Cabinet which is responsible for the fact that Russia has not become a total anarchist state; for only six weeks have passed since the *coup d'état*, and if it is ever toppled by all those different kinds of Socialists, including those Pacifists arriving from Switzerland via Germany, then the future looks bad. Any extreme left ministry will be born dead, for it is very possible that at that moment a General X on a white charger will come riding along. . . .

While the negotiations between the Duma and the Soviet were in progress, the question of the future of the Tsar and the Romanoffs was discussed. The Duma leaders were against Russia becoming a republic, and they wanted above all to save the monarchy and the dynasty.

Guchkov and Shulgin, two of the more conservative members were sent to the Tsar's headquarters at Pskov to try to obtain the Tsar's abdication in favour of his son with the Grand Duke Michael as regent. At first the Tsar had signed the manifesto of abdication, but a little later he changed his mind. He had realized that Alexis, as infant Tsar, would have been taken away from him to complete his education elsewhere, and this Nicholas could not accept. So another Deed of Abdication was drawn up and which Nicholas signed; this time he abdicated, not only on his own behalf, but also on behalf of his sickly son in favour of his brother Michael.

Michael and Natasha had been continuing to live their usual way of life these past months in spite of the unrest and revolutionary stirrings in Petrograd. Here is a typical entry in Michael's diary:

> 15th January 1917. Natasha and I went to church at 11 a.m. Princess Putyatin and the Tolstoys came to lunch. We all went for a drive in sleighs in the afternoon to the Game Reserve and the Priorate. Alesha [Matveiev] arrived at 2 p.m. We went to Johnson's at 4.15 and had tea, and afterwards we had some music – Johnson played the piano, the Princess sang and Dominichi and I played our guitars. At 6 p.m. the Tolstoys left and we went home. Then Dvorjitsky came to dinner and stayed until 11 p.m. Princess Putyatin and Tata went to bed at 9.45. Weather was at times quite sunny. 5°.

Natasha had endowed three hospitals for wounded soldiers, one at Gatchina, one at Lvov and one at Kiev, and this meant that she had been quite busy superintending their running, as all the costs were paid out of her own pocket. They had heard of the murder of Rasputin, and had been in mixed minds about it; Michael abhorred violence above all else, and could not approve of the method which had been taken to remove Rasputin. Michael had been one of the people who had begged Grand Duke Nicholas to write to the Tsar about the danger of that mad monk, but had never imagined murder being committed. Natasha, on the other hand, was openly pleased that Rasputin had been removed, and did not care by what means this removal had been accomplished.

Gradually, as January passed and February arrived, the entries in Michael's diary began to change. No longer did they chronicle the family's social engagements to such an extent, but now he was detailing other happenings as well:

> 3rd February 1917. (In the train from the front to Gatchina.) We are three hours late arriving, probably due to snow drifts. I write 'probably' as one can never find out the real truth. But the fact is that everything is in complete disorder everywhere.

> 25th February 1917. There were disorders on the Nevsky Propekt today. Workers were going around waving red flags and throwing grenades and bottles at the police, which compelled the troops to open fire. The main cause of the unrest is the shortage of flour in the shops.

> 26th February 1917. The riots in Petrograd have increased in size. On the Suvorov Pospekt and Znamensky Street 200 people were killed.

But Michael and Natasha continued to entertain their friends as of old. A few servants had left in a hurry without giving notice, but that was all. Their old friend Dimitri Abrikossow was one of the guests during this period, and he wrote a poignant description of two of these get-togethers:

> ... I remember how I arrived in Gatchina one time and was at once taken to a small hunting lodge, hidden in the woods, where a magnificent supper was served. Gypsies were singing, and much wine was drunk. I tried to escape from the orgy, but it was dark and cold outside and I did not know my way back. The only man who shared my gloom was Grand Duke Michael, but he bowed to the wishes of his wife, who liked crowds and flattery. Another time, when the same people decided to go for a drive, I declined on the pretext that I should remain with Grand Duke Michael, who was not well.
>
> Whenever I think of this lovable man and his sad fate, I see him as I saw him that Sunday. The house was very quiet, everybody else having gone out; he did not wish any light, though dusk had come early and we faced each other in the twilight. Lying on a couch, shivering from fever, he talked in a sad voice about the difficulty of living among the sorrows, wickedness, selfishness and deceitfulness of men, and that God was far away. He told me that he often thought how difficult it was for his brother, who sincerely wanted to do only what was good for the people, but who was hindered by his wife. Several times he had tried to convey to Nicholas what people were saying about him and about the dangerous influence of the Empress; Nicholas seemed indifferent to his fate, leaving everything in the hands of God, but under the influence of Rasputin God had assumed a strange shape; Michael was afraid of the future. I tried to console him, but could not find words equal to the intensity of his grief. Tears choked his voice. It had become quite dark. When I turned on the light I was shocked by the utter despair on the pale face before me and had the distinct feeling that we all stood on the threshold of great misfortune. At that moment our gay party returned and my only intimate conversation with the Grand Duke was ended.

That winter Michael came to the conclusion that he should try to 'do something' and see if he could not in some way ease the precarious political situation, and he went to Petrograd to see Rodzyanko. It was agreed that a compromise might well be the answer, and that it should take the form of a Constitutional Monarchy, headed nominally by the infant Alexis under the regency of Michael. Michael had agreed to this in principle, but the discussions were to be kept quite secret and not even the other members of the Romanoffs had been told. Michael wrote in his diary:

27th February 1917. At 5 p.m. Johnson and I took a special train and went to Petrograd. In the Marinsky Palace we met M.N. Rodzyanko, Nekrassoff, Savich and Dimitriukoff, and later we were joined by Prince Galitzine, General Beliaieff and Kryzhanovsky. When we arrived in Petrograd, things were comparatively quiet, but by 8 p.m. shooting began in the streets and almost all the armed forces went over to the side of the revolutionaries, and order ceased to exist. A temporary Executive Committee was formed which began to issue orders; this was made up of several members of the Duma, headed by their President, Rodzyanko. I went straight to the War Ministry and sent a telegram direct to General Alexeiev at Mogilev to pass on to Nicky. In it I enumerated the measures that should be taken immediately to stop the revolution that has already begun. For instance, the resignation of the whole of the Cabinet Ministers, and that Prince Lvov should form a new Cabinet of his own choice, and that the answer must be given at once as the matter was of the utmost urgency – every hour counts. In due course the answer came: 'You must make no changes whatsoever until I arrive. My departure is fixed for 2.30 p.m. tomorrow.' Alas. After this unsuccessful attempt to help I decided to return home to Gatchina, but this was not possible owing to heavy machine-gun fire and grenade explosions in the streets. At 3 a.m. things had quietened down a little, and Johnson and I decided to drive our car along Gorokhovaia Street with an escort, then along the quay as far as the Nicholas Bridge. Then we turned left hoping to reach the railway station, but we saw that this was too dangerous as revolutionary detachments were patrolling everywhere and at one point we were nearly stopped, but we accelerated and managed to get away but our escort was stopped and arrested. We decided that we should go no further and we went back to the Winter Palace. There we found General Beliaiev and General Khabaloff who had a force of 1000 troops. I was able to persuade the two generals not to defend the Palace and they decided to evacuate it before dawn and thus avoid the inevitable destruction of it by the revolutionaries. Poor General K. was very grateful to me for such advice. At 5 a.m. Johnson and I left the Palace and walked to Princess Putyatin's house and went to sleep on some couches.

28th February 1917. We were awakened by the sound of heavy traffic, cars and lorries filled with soldiers shooting in the air, and the noise of hand grenades exploding. The soldiers were shouting and cheering, waving red flags and wearing red ribbons and rosettes in their button holes and pinned to their chests. But the day passed peacefully for us and no one came and bothered us.

1st March 1917. In the morning some of the apartments in Putyatin's house were searched by revolutionaries, but not ours, and Princess Putyatin was very worried. At 12.30 a deputation consisting of several officers together with a lawyer called Ivanoff came to see me. They asked me to sign a proposed Manifesto to which my uncles P. and K. had already put their signatures. This Manifesto announced that the Tsar was granting a full constitution. Later on I wrote a letter to Rodzyanko. All day there was the sound of heavy traffic like yesterday and there was some shooting; at one point the Preobazhensky Regiment marched past with the band playing. We heard about some murders committed by soldiers. Nicky should have arrived from his HQ at the front, but has not, and no one knows exactly where his train is at the moment. Some say that it is at Bologoe. All the power is now in the hands of the Temporary Committee who are in difficulties because of strong pressure from the Committee of Deputies of Workers and Soldiers. Rodzyanko should have come to see me but was prevented.

2nd March 1917. In the morning I received a reply from Rodzyanko. We were left quite undisturbed today. Heavy movement of traffic continues but the shooting has stopped. Nevertheless I must add that there is complete insubordination in the ranks of the army and total anarchy reigns.

That day, the 2nd March was the day that Nicholas signed his Manifesto of Abdication. After signing it, he sent a telegram to Michael:

To His Majesty the Emperor Michael: Recent events have forced me to decide irrevocably to take this extreme step. Forgive me if it grieves you and also for no warning – there was no time. Shall always remain a faithful and devoted brother. Now returning to HQ where hope to come back shortly to Tsarskoe Selo. Fervently pray God to help you and our country.

Nicky.

Though Michael had been heir to the throne for many years before the birth of Alexis, and during the latter's long periods of illness had been aware of the possibility that he might again become the Heir Apparent, he had never imagined that Nicholas would abdicate so suddenly and hand him (Michael) directly the throne of Russia.

So at 6 a.m. on the 3rd March Michael was woken up by a telephone call from Kerensky advising him that the complete Council of Ministers were going to visit him in an hour's time, at 7 a.m. 'Actually they arrived only at 9.30 a.m.' was the only comment Michael made in his diary about this momentous day of his life when he was offered the throne.

Before Kerensky and the other Ministers arrived, Michael telephoned Natasha at home at Gatchina from the Putyatin's flat, Natasha was 'beside herself', but it was not from excitement at the idea of becoming the consort of an Emperor; for whatever has been said or written about her, no one has ever accused her of being stupid, and it would have been an extremely stupid person who felt no terror at the idea of their husband's wearing the crown of Imperial Russia in those dangerous and terrible times. As the news spread through her household the servants stopped their work and stood about exclaiming and crying among themselves; food was left to burn unheeded on the stoves, the children ran around shouting in excitement until sent to their nurseries to be out of the way; the telephone bell shrilled unceasingly, and all the dogs barked non-stop. The Russian temperament is such that even a small domestic crisis provokes much shouting and rushing about and gesticulating, so that everyone, right down to the humblest stable-boy was in a state of hysteria that day.

Nicholas's Manifesto of Abdication read:

> In this great struggle with a foreign enemy, who for nearly three years has tried to enslave our country, the Lord God has been pleased to send down on Russia a new heavy trial. The internal popular disturbances which have begun, threaten to have a disastrous effect on the future conduct of this persistent war. The destiny of Russia, the honour of our heroic army, the good of the people, the

whole future of our dear country demand that whatever it cost, the war should be brought to a victorious end.

The cruel enemy is gathering his last forces, and already the hour is near when our gallant army, together with our glorious allies, will be able finally to crush the enemy.

In these decisive days in the life of Russia, we have thought it a duty of conscience to facilitate for our people a close union and consolidation of all national forces for the speedy attainment of victory; and, in agreement with the Imperial Duma, we have thought it good to abdicate from the throne of the Russian State, and to lay down the supreme power.

Not wishing to part with our dear son we hand over our inheritance to our brother, the Grand Duke Michael Alexandrovitch, and give him our blessing to mount to throne of the Russian State. We bequeath it to our brother to direct the forces of the State in full and inviolable union with the representatives of the people in the legislative institutions, on those principles which will by then be established.

In the name of our dearly loved country we call on all faithful sons of the Fatherland to fulfill their sacred duty to him by obedience to the Tsar at a heavy moment of national trials, to help him, together with the representatives of the people, to bring the Russian State onto the road of victory, prosperity and glory.

May the Lord God help Russia!

Nicholas.

There were many prophecies about the Romanoffs, but there were two which were especially popular. The first one said that the Romanoff Dynasty, having started with a Michael, would finish with a Michael. The second predicted that when Michael II reigned, Russia would conquer Constantinople. Now there was a Michael II, the only Tsar Michael since Michael I in 1613, the first of the Romanoffs. Which of these prophecies would prove to be true?

In Petrograd, as Michael waited there to face the Soviet, there were disagreements. Milyukov, Gutchkov and Shulgin all thought that there must be a Tsar, that the monarchy was the one thing that unified Russia, and that without it she would be lost; they believed that Michael must face up to his responsibilities and ascend the throne. On the other hand, Rodzyanko and Kerensky argued that Michael's ascension would be against the will of the people and would only provoke a new wave of unrest and revolution. Michael entered the room in Prince Putyatin's apartment where the meeting was in progress. Shulgin wrote later: 'The Grand Duke, a tall youngish man with a pale face, looking the very picture of fragility, sat in an armchair in a private drawing room, surrounded by the new ministers. . . .' He listened to all the arguments which were put before him. It was quite clear to everyone that the Grand Duke could only have reigned for a few hours as his ascension would have precipitated colossal bloodshed in the capital leading to general civil war. Also it was pointed out that Michael would have been killed immediately as he had no reliable troops at his disposal at that time. Rodzyanko wrote later: 'The Grand Duke asked me outright whether I could guarantee his life if he acceded to the throne, and I had to answer in the negative.' Michael left the room to decide what to do. Five minutes was all the time he needed to make a decision. He returned and announced that he would abdicate in his turn.

At this very moment, V. D. Nabokov was hurrying

through the streets. In his book *The Provisional Government* he describes how he received a telephone message that day asking him to go at once to Prince Putyatin's apartment. 'The Nevsky presented an extraordinary spectacle: there wasn't a single carriage or car, there were no police, and there were crowds of people occupying the breadth of the street. In front of the Anichkov Palace they were burning eagles which had been taken down from the signs of court-appointed victuallers. . . .' When he arrived at the apartment he asked Prince Lvov why he had been asked to come, and was told that they were having trouble with the drawing-up of Michael's deed of abdication. The deed had been drafted by Nekrasov, but it was not entirely successful, and as everybody was terribly tired they were no longer able to think straight. They had been up all the previous night, and they badly needed help with the final text. Nabokov immediately asked permission to telephone a lawyer friend of his, a Baron Nolde, and as soon as he heard what was wanted from him, he came hurrying over from the Ministry of Foreign Affairs where he had been. They were assigned a room belonging to Prince Putyatin's daughter, and together with Shulgin, they settled down to draw up a new deed of abdication. Eventually, after a great deal of discussion and hard work, they completed a draft which satisfied them; the text was copied out by Nabokov, and shown to Michael. He proposed some alterations; a reference to God (which had been missing), and in the address to the people the words 'I command' were to be replaced by the words 'I request'. So Nabokov had to copy out the document once more. By this time it was six o'clock, and Rodzyanko arrived. Michael read the final version of the deed and approved of it.

In drawing up this deed, its authors found themselves in a quandary. Should it be considered that, at that moment, Michael was already Emperor? Should the deed be the same sort as the one which had been signed by Nicholas? But if so, then might not the other members of the Imperial family become involved in succession rights? Furthermore, had Nicholas the right to name his brother as Emperor at all? So they decided to interpret the situation as follows: that Michael was refusing to assume the supreme Authority, and by refusing he recognized the full powers of the Provisional Government and its continuity with the State Duma.

So Michael signed the deed. Nabokov writes: 'He appeared to be rather awkward and somewhat embarrassed. I have no doubt that it was very painful for him, but he retained complete self-control, although I must confess I do not think he fully realized the importance and significance of what he was doing. Before we adjourned he and M. V. Rodzyanko embraced and kissed, and Rodzyanko called him a most noble man.'

In signing this deed of abdication, Michael swept away a dynasty which had lasted for three hundred and four years; so the first of the ancient prophecies was the true one. The Romanoff dynasty was no more.

9 Vortex

Eventually Michael made his way home to Natasha. He wrote the following entry in his diary:

> 4th March 1917. At 11 a.m. Johnson and I went to Baltic Station escorted by two officers and followed by another car containing cadets armed with rifles. On the way General Yusefovitch joined us. The station was packed with soldiers and everywhere one could see machine guns and boxes of ammunition. I travelled in a special train with Johnson and Yusefovitch. Before the train left a military detachment lined up outside my carriage and I saluted them, and the crowd which had gathered cheered me. We arrived at Gatchina at 1.30 and I sighed with relief when at last I was home. The Grand Duke George Mikhailovitch* will be staying with us from Tuesday – he has just arrived from the front and asked me if he could stay with us. I hear that order in general is being re-established.

Slowly life returned to more or less normal. Michael spent much of the days lying on a chaise-longue – all the strain of the past weeks had exhausted him and he was not feeling well. On 6th March, Serge Cheremetevsky, Natasha's father, came to visit them and brought news of conditions in Moscow. He reported that everything had gone quietly there and that there had been no bloodshed. In Petrograd the mood was improving and

---

* Brother of Grand Duke Nicholas Mikailovitch.

order was being re-established; cabs were once more to be seen in the streets and trams were due to start running again the next day. Discipline, though, especially in the army, was non-existent. In Gatchina it seemed almost as if the last weeks had just been a bad dream, all the talk of 'abdication manifesto' faded away. When Natasha went out, her sleigh was still decorated with its usual white rosette and there were some people who still bowed as she passed by, even though other sleighs carried red rosettes. On Sunday 12th March, Michael noted in his diary:

> At 11 a.m. Natasha, Tata and I went to church. A disgusting red flag was swinging on the Palace tower. There were rumours that the occupants have requested that the two-headed eagle should be removed from the cupola, but happily this did not happen. These last few days there has been the sound of heavy firing from the game reserve and a great many deer were killed. The gunmen were soldiers from various units. Bullets were even reaching the town. Fortunately there was a round-up of these hunters yesterday and this slaughter and hooliganism were stopped.

In his Palace in Petrograd the Grand Duke Nicholas Mikhailovitch was writing to his friends in Paris:

> ... If I am elected to the famous Constitutional Assembly, I will vote for a Republic. And this is why! Who are the candidates for a Monarchy? First of all, the Grand Duke Michael. He is another edition of his brother without the learning of Nicholas, without a bit of character, and married to a woman from the legal world of Moscow. She was married twice before, and that does not count her love affairs. This Natasha Cheremetevsky is an intelligent but evil woman, and her friends are interlopers and shady characters. The next candidate is Cyril, a pompous idiot, but he has a wife who is a charming and great lady (they have two daughters, no son as yet.). Then there is the man,

that Music-Hall lover, that Boris, who is well-known in Paris. Finally we have André the Gigolo, the lover of my brother's mistress, the dancer. To Hell with all of them! . . . No thanks! I would personally prefer Nicholas II, but as he would never repudiate the woman of Hesse, then NO. And so it is that I am led to prefer an authoritative Republic with a President eligible for four years only, as seven years would be too long a period for us Russians with our changing tastes and varying appetites! . . .

As the weather improved and the snow melted, and as it became possible once more to stroll in the streets, hooligans began to break into Michael's garden after dark. In the mornings the gardeners would find that plants and shrubs had been damaged, and that the garden had been used as a public lavatory. So a company of cadets from the Military Academy were detailed to patrol the grounds at night. The governess continued to give Tata her lessons, and after Michael's health improved, he and Tata decided to carry on with their rides, but now they kept mostly to the parks. That summer they often went for drives in the Rolls Royce with their visitors, and sometimes they even went for picnics as in the old days. Food was still fairly easy to obtain in Gatchina, though prices had risen quite a lot, and they were able to entertain their guests in more or less the usual style, for they still came from Petrograd and from Moscow.

On 26th May Johnson received a deputation of a Soviet of soldiers, workers and peasants from Tsarskoe Selo. They had come to establish the exact number of cars owned by Michael. But that summer passed peacefully enough in Gatchina. Up to then there had been absolutely no hostile demonstrations at all by the people. It is true that law and order had been relaxed to a certain extent – men could be seen to spit out sunflower seed husks on to the footpaths, something that had been forbidden before. Occasionally there were rowdy meetings held at street corners; sometimes at night the sound of sporadic shooting could be heard, and there were a few acts of minor hooliganism; families took to strolling in the hitherto reserved parks, but there was no serious trouble, and the mood was generally peaceful.

On 21st August, at about 7 p.m., Michael's garden was suddenly surrounded by a lot of soldiers under the command of two officers. Then Captain Kosmin, the Assistant Commander-in-Chief of the Petrograd district arrived accompanied by Captain Svistunov, the Gatchina Commandant. They announced that by order of the Minister of the Interior and the Minister of War, Michael was to be put under house arrest forthwith. They produced the following document and gave it to Michael:

> To the Commander-in-Chief of all Forces of the Petrograd District:
>> Based on the resolution of the Temporary Government of 2nd August 1917, an order has been made to arrest the former Grand Duke Michael Alexandrovitch as a person whose activities are a threat to the defence of the country and to the safety of the freedom gained by the revolution. This person must be kept under the strictest house arrest under a specially instructed guard. This order must be declared to the former Grand Duke, who is to be kept under arrest until further notice.
>> Signed. Director of War Ministry.
>> Savinkoff.

When Natasha and Johnson, who had been shopping, arrived from Petrograd half an hour later, Kosmin also put them under house arrest, and they were made to sign a form of agreement. After that Kosmin and Svistunoff left, leaving the family under guard. Michael wrote in his diary the next day:

> Our guard is 60–70 strong. The sentries are posted on the outer parts of our garden and on the outside of the fence. We have just read the news in the papers of our arrest. . . .

On the 23rd August, before lunch, Michael wrote to Kerensky complaining of being arrested and asking permission for him and his family to go abroad. That afternoon Captain Kosmin brought Kerensky's verbal reply; this was to the effect that though he (Kerensky) had personally no doubt of Michael's loyalty, the present situation made it absolutely necessary to keep Michael isolated. As to the question of going abroad, he was afraid that it was impossible for the time being. The diary entry for 25th August reads as follows:

> We spent the whole day indoors. It was declared to us that during our strolls in the garden we shall be accompanied by a non-commissioned officer, and we decided not to go out any more for the present. . . .

Then on 28th August, General Korniloff attempted a military coup. He had formed an army and was marching on Petrograd and Gatchina to 'liberate' the Whites. Michael describes what happened:

> 29th August 1917. I was woken up at 3 a.m. and the Commandant told us that we should prepare for departure, and to be ready in one hour's time. We all managed to be

ready in time, but did not leave until 5.10 as the army drivers had trouble starting up our cars. Eventually they had to wake up our chauffeur Vedikhoff, which we had advised them to do in the first place. The journey took ages and at long last we arrived in Petrograd, at 9 p.m. only. On the way we saw the Preobajensky Reserve marching in the direction of Petrograd, obviously on their way to help defend the city. When we arrived, we were taken to the office of the Commander-in-Chief of the Petrograd District and were met by Captain Filonenko. From there we were taken to an address in Morskaya Street but the accommodation was completely unsuitable – no elementary comforts and only three beds. Fortunately, after endless discussions and with Johnson's help, we went to Alesha's flat on the Fontanka. We immediately put the children to bed, and we went to bed ourselves at 11 p.m. My stomach pains are worse. We are guarded by 65 soldiers and are under strict arrest. We read in the papers that Kornilov's coup is doomed to failure.

30th August 1917. I spent the whole day in bed. Alesha called in the morning and we talked in the Commandant's presence. We are all very tired and nervous. Today's news: General Kornilov's advance towards Petrograd has been stopped. The Temporary Government have arrested General Denikin and markoff, but Kornilov has been suspended and it is declared that he will be brought to trial.

31st August 1917. I spent the day partly in an armchair and partly in bed. The duty officer is in the next room and two guards are placed by the front door. That is how we dangerous criminals are guarded! Today's news: Kornilov's coup is over. The General himself is starting negotiations with the Temporary Government over his surrender. Kerensky has assumed supreme command, General Alexeev being his Chief of Staff. We cannot find out what is to become of us and we feel frustrated and miserable. Vedhikoff came yesterday and today from

The Empress Elizabeth Petrovna built the Pietrovski Palace which was once used as a headquarters by Napoleon. When Natasha was a young girl it was a favourite pleasure ground for Muscovites in the summer months.

Sergei Mamontoff, Natasha's first husband, and the author's grandfather, was a member of the wealthy Moscow family who were famous patrons of art.

Natasha and her daughter Tata in Gatchina soon after Natasha's second husband, Liolocha Wulfert, was posted to the Blue Cuirassiers.

The Grand Duke Michael Alexandrovitch, younger brother of the Tsar Nicholas II, in his uniform as Colonel-in-Chief of the Blue Cuirassiers, and like the one of his brother, in national costume.

The earliest photograph of Natasha and Misha in Gatchina soon after they first met.

Misha and his sister, the Grand Duchess Olga, shared the secrets of their love affairs; his with Natasha and hers with Nikolai Koulikovsky.

The Grand Duke and two of his many pets.
This studio double portrait photograph was taken soon after Misha and Natasha were married.

Exiled and free at last to be happily married, Michael cavorts on holiday in Switzerland.

The obligatory pose on the obligatory Alpine climb in obligatory costume.

The hazards of a motoring holiday before the first World War.

Luncheon in the South of France.

Baby George and Mamma in the South of France.

Exiled to England and domiciled at Knebworth; stately home, stately lawns and Russian wolfhound.

At Knebworth; just about to leave for London and a night at the Royal Opera.

The library in Knebworth in which can be seen the urn (to the right) now in the author's possession.

Christmas for the children on the estate at Knebworth.

Misha, Tata, George and 'Beauty' at Knebworth.

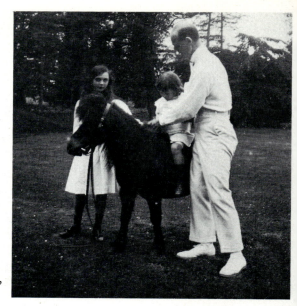

Exiles return. The small lake at the Gatchina estate, 1915.

One of the drawing rooms in Brassowo, 1915.

Teatime at Gatchina. Misha's faithful Johnson is at the extreme right.

Dimitri Abrikossov and the Grand Duke became close friends during the war.

The Grand Duke Nicholas Mikhailovitch, Misha's uncle, with captured Austrian troops.

Brassowo in early Spring, 1916.

Natasha and the Grand Duke Dimitri Pavlovitch at Brassowo early in the year before he joined Prince Felix Youssopoff in the assassination of Rasputin.

Part of the Brassowo estate in 1916.   Young George's letter to his father who he never saw again.

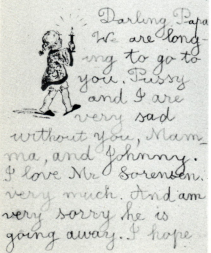

Darling Papa
We are longing to go to you. Pussy and I are very sad without you, Mamma, and Johnny. I love Mr Sorensen very much. And am very sorry he is going away. I hope you are quite well. Will you let us go to Bratzuika. Best love and kisses to Papa and Johnny.

The Grand Duke with S. I. Ossovetsky and A. S. Matvieieff inspecting the Dux hangar at the Moscow airfield.

The last photograph of Misha taken in custody in Perm.

Tata's passport issued in September, 1918.

Tata's release paper from the Cheka prison, signed by commissars **Boki** and Apanasevitch.

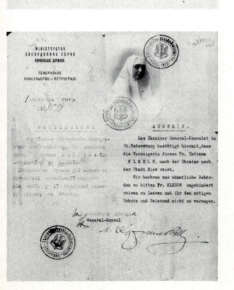

Disguised as a nursing sister and assuming the name Tatania Klenow, Natasha was granted this permit to enter the Ukraine.

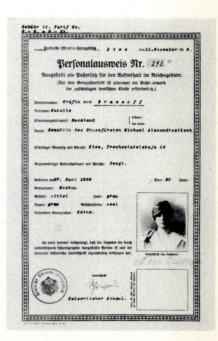

2nd November, 1918, the German authorities in the Ukraine granted Natasha a passport enabling her to leave Russia.

Aboard *HMS Neride* after the misunderstanding had been cleared up—when Natasha and her friend had been taken for ladies of the town. Constantinople en route to Malta and then to England.

Constantinople en route to Malta and then to England.

The Grand Duchess Xenia Alexandrovna.

After the revolution the Russian Embassy in London was known as 'Russian House'. After 1919 it was used by the Russian emigrés as a meeting place for functions like this one in 1925. The Grand Duchess Xenia is at the right on the bottom step, and Natasha behind her, four steps up.

George and one of his motor bikes.   George.

England, 1928. Cecil Gray, the author's father; Mme Diamantidi, Natasha, Tata (the author's mother) and George.

The special *certificat d'identité* issued to Russian exiles in France in the 30s. These were invalidated if the bearer were to enter the USSR.

The South of France in the mid-30s.

After the visit by an unknown Soviet official, Natasha and George's grave in Passy was refurbished thanks to the Parisian Russian community.

Colonel Michael Goleniewski who claims to be the Tsarevitch Alexes and a survivor of the Russian Imperial family, photographed recently in New York.

Gatchina in the Rolls Royce and brought us some personal belongings, provisions and some flowers. A cabinet of 5 has been formed: Kerensky, Tereshchenko, Nikitine, Veshinsky and Verderevsky. My stomach pains are worse.

1st September 1917. I spent the day in bed. Professor Vestfalen arrived from Finland and examined me. He has diagnosed a stomach ulcer, and has prescribed a strict diet of milk and dry biscuit every two hours and application of a hot water bottle. The ulcer is caused by nervous strain brought on by my arrest.

2nd September 1917. . . . . We woke up today to hear the news that Russia is declared a Democratic Republic. Isn't it all the same whatever form of government there is, as long as there is order and justice for all?

4th September 1917 . . . the only proper treatment for my ulcer is a strict diet, hot water bottles, and above all, complete moral and physical rest. But where can one find these in the present circumstances?

6th September 1917 . . . Captain Kosmin arrived at 5 p.m. It has been decided to move us back to Gatchina. Our departure was delayed until 10 p.m. as Kosmin had to have Kerensky's instructions from his HQ about our journey. Our *cortège* consisted of five cars, two of them ours. First came two cars with our luggage and servants, then Natasha, children, I and Kosmin in the Packard; behind us Miss Neame, Johnson and the Commandant; and bringing up the rear was our Rolls Royce containing the guards. As soon as we arrived, I went to bed. It is so nice to be back home at last.

In less than a week after arriving home Michael's ulcer began to heal, and he reports his improvement in health in his diary. On 13th September Captain Kosmin visited him and told him that they were now freed from their arrest. 'But why' Michael wrote 'were we arrested in the first place? Nobody knows, and naturally there were no charges made, in fact none could possibly have been made. But where is the guarantee that this is not going to happen again one day?' Two days later Captain Kosmin arrived unexpectedly, and gave Michael a written permit from Kerensky to go to the Crimea whenever they wished. But Michael never availed himself of this permission; why he did not is not known. . . .

By now things had changed in Gatchina; there was an atmosphere of tension; everyone was talking about Lenin; at night there was the sound of firing and during the day the noise of shouting and general disorder. The house was guarded by uncouth youths who tramped all over the place and pillaged the garden. From time to time Michael was ordered to Petrograd for questioning by the authorities. Again and again he went; again and again he was allowed to return home safely. One day Michael's 'devoted' valet, a man named Baranoff who had been with him for years suddenly ran off. A young man called Vassili Chelicheff, who had been Michael's batman at the front, was given the post and was very moved and honoured by the promotion.

One day Natasha asked permission to go to Petrograd to visit her bank; she pretended that she wished to examine some important papers, though in fact her aim was to rescue some of her jewels which had been confiscated when the bank had been seized by the government. Though an official stayed by her the whole time she was there, she nevertheless managed to cram a considerable amount of the more valuable pieces into her fur muff, and returned home safely, unmolested.

10 October and Onwards

The Grand Duke Nicholas Mikhailovitch was still living in his Palace in Petrograd and was still writing his long letters to his friend Frederic Masson in Paris. His letters of October and November 1917 show him to be an extremely astute elderly gentleman who saw everything and missed nothing. At the beginning of October 1917 he wrote:

> Anarchy is total and no one can say when this state of affairs will end . . . . Bolshevism is winning in the countryside, and certain areas are being completely devastated by peasants and army deserters. A number of estates are already ruined, and not only those belonging to the middle class and 'aristos' but also those of the peasants, some of whom possessed some beautiful properties. No one is spared and everything is burned and pillaged. The Provisional Government is incapable of controlling this storm as the soldiers are themselves the destructive elements, therefore who is to keep law and order? . . .
>
> . . . The seed of disorganization and disorder has had time to take root, and now really only the arrival of Ivan the Terrible could put an end to this diabolical orgy which is devastating the whole country, and which is covering Russia with shame and dishonour in the eyes of our dear allies. But in Russia even the impossible can happen, and I do not want to believe that this *danse macabre* will go on and

on. And winter has only just started! This means that there will be a new series of atrocities once Russia is covered with snow. We must be patient and bear our new woes with courage and hope that all this will soon come to an end, and that such a state of affairs cannot last for ever.

At the beginnning of November he wrote the following:

> The filthy band of Bolsheviks stop at nothing, and as they are penniless, they seize the State Bank and the others as well. Due credit must be given to the bank clerks who try their utmost to withstand them, but alas, many millions have already been taken by Trotsky, Lenin and Co. How much longer must we bear this intolerable yoke, nobody knows, and I see no light of salvation at all. It is worse than the Terror with its guillotine, but as these gentlemen have abolished the death penalty, they permit escaped prisoners, in other words professional bandits and assassins, to murder people in the streets and in their homes . . . .
>
> To give you an idea of our daily life, listen to the following: while I write this, bands of soldiers (un-armed) are pillaging the cellars of the Winter Palace. This started at midnight and continued all through the night. Now it is 10 a.m. and all the neighbouring streets, the Court Quay, the Millionaya Street, the Square of the Winter Palace, the Stable Street, are full of drunken soldiers who do no actual harm but who do everything else, things that I cannot bring myself to describe to you. Horrified and disgusted on-lookers, those passers-by going about their own affairs, cannot understand the reason for this mob of drunks at this hour in the morning . . . .

The Grand Duke Nicholas had been a fervent admirer of Kerensky, and in September had written to M. Masson that he feared for Kerensky, as he was being attacked on all sides:

> . . . Remember that the day he is no more, the safety of the

exiles in Siberia, of those in the Crimea and of us all, will be doubtful; and that Anarchy will increase with the likelihood of a civil war all over Russia ....

Then what the Grand Duke had been fearing, happened. Kerensky fell. Grand Duke Nicholas wrote:

... The 25 Oct/7 Nov. bands of Bolsheviks laid seige to the Winter Palace; shooting lasted all night and towards dawn on the 26th October the Palace fell and all the Ministers were taken on foot to the fortress. Only Kerensky was able to escape in a car which an American lent him at the last minute. ... At the moment Kerensky is fleeing, no one knows to where, and an armistice has been reached between the two sides. ...

At the end of October Natasha started to pack some of their more valuable items in chests, to be taken away and hidden. On 1st November Michael wrote in his diary:

At 3.30 Natasha and I drove to the Game Reserve where we went for a walk and then heard the sound of shooting. We returned to our car and heard loud voices and saw that there were some soldiers at the gates. Suddenly there was a loud report – evidently some scoundrel shot in our direction. When we arrived home Johnson told us that Kerensky had just escaped from the Palace. ... All Gatchina is surrounded by Bolshevik forces and they are searching everywhere for Kerensky ... two of our cars were confiscated.

2nd November 1917. At 5 p.m. the Engineer Rakinsky arrived and took away our last remaining car and even wanted to arrest us. Later it transpired that he acted without any authority and that he was severly reprimanded.

3rd November 1917. ... It is comparatively quiet in Petrograd but in Moscow they say that there is real war. The Uspensky and the St. Basil cathedrals, together with the Town Hall, are destroyed; a great part of Moscow is on fire and there are many dead and wounded.

The next day, 4th November, Michael was ordered by the Military Revolutionary Committee to go to the Smolny Institute in Petrograd for his own safety. After long discussions it was agreed that he could go and stay instead with his friends, the Putyatins. So Natasha and Michael spent several days there, and eventually returned to Gatchina. During the morning of the 23rd November some airmen from the Flying School appeared and confiscated eighty bottles of Michael's wine and a quantity of sugar. Some of the wine was drunk on the spot, and some bottles were smashed.

Christmas came and then soon it was the New Year once more. But this year everyone was too worried and depressed to feel like celebrating, though of course the children were given presents as usual. There was still, even now, quite a steady stream of visitors from Petrograd, and Natasha was always pleased to see them, as she felt that they were a welcome distraction for Michael; they helped him recover his spirits a little. On 11th January 1918 there appeared an article in one of the papers which Michael copied down in his diary:

DESTRUCTION OF THE ARMY

Chief-of-Staff of the Supreme Commander, General Bonch-Bruevitch has sent the following telegram to the Glavcoverk Krylenko:

Complete Anarchy. Many parts of the Front are uncovered. At the Western Front there are only 160 armed men to the verst. There are no reserves to replace soldiers in the trenches. Most of the experienced commanders were left out of the elections and the present commanding officers are without experience. Very soon all Staffs will automatically stop working as there is no one to operate them. The General Staff does not exist any more and the conditions of work are impossible. The economy is completely dislocated. The training and order are almost non-existant. Orders are not executed. There is mass desertion. Those on leave never return. Inter-communication is non-existent. Horses are completely annihilated. The fortified positions go to ruin. Barbed wire fences are removed for the ease of fraternization and commerce. Any onslaught from the enemy would be impossible to withstand. The only salvation of the army would be withdrawal to natural defence lines. . . .

The war was as good as lost; no country could have a revolution and win a war at the same time. It only remained for a peace treaty to be signed – a peace treaty that was to prove humiliating for Russia.

Every few weeks Michael was summoned to Petrograd for 'questioning' by the new Commissar of the Petrograd Soviet, Uritsky. The Grand Duke Nicholas Mikhailovitch had written amusingly to M. Masson in Paris about this man. His letter is dated 11/24 December, 1917:

. . . a Jew named Uritsky who was convicted of theft and smuggling during the war and was imprisoned in Copenhagen, and who, on release, was expelled from Denmark. At the moment he is one of the more influential Commissars and is head of the Counter-Revolutionary Group. He has a fanatical hatred of the Romanoffs and I would love to tell you in detail of my three conversations with this peasant who pretends to be a Fouquier-Tinville and who quotes at every possible moment (impossible ones too!) the example of the great French Revolution. In spite of my cool head the third conversation ended with my bursting out laughing which astonished him very much. He had announced to me with great pomp and circumstance that a Travel Permit would be given to us for any country we required just as soon as the Proletariat had replaced the current Government. Then I quietly asked for a permit to go to Denmark; it was a terrible blunder on my part as I knew very well that he had served his sentence in Danish prisons. This brought forth his rage and a delicious monologue on the political exiles of 1789–1792. . . . To think that Russia has fallen so low as to be ruled by all these low '*Youpins.*'

One cold bright morning in early March Michael was writing up his diary for the previous day. He was writing:

At 10.15 Vassily and I came home from Johnson's. Before lunch and after, until 4 p.m. I sat on the children's balcony although it was not as warm as yesterday – there was a light wind. Olga P. was sitting with me. After tea Olga P. returned to Petrograd by the Warsaw train. Natasha and Boris went for a walk and visited the Cottons, and we, Margaret, V. and I, had some music. She played the mandolin and I accompanied her on the guitar, until 7.30. In the evening. . . .

That is the last thing that Michael wrote in his diary, for while he was writing those last words he received a summons to go once again to Petrograd to the Smolny Institute, for yet another interrogation by Uritsky. Natasha was not unduly worried to see him go, for had he not invariably returned safely from these trips, time and time again? But this time it was different. Michael sent a note from the Smolny to Natasha, scribbled on a rough piece of paper:

My dear Natasha,
Uritsky has just read us the resolution of the Soviet of People's Commissars declaring that we have to move

immediately to Perm. They gave us half-an-hour to get ready. Uritsky assures me that you and the family will have no difficulty in following whenever you wish. We are going as far as Perm all together, but there, according to the order of the Soviet of the P.C., we part with N.N., as he is ordered not to live in the same town as myself for at least one month. Please make arrangements to send to Perm anyone you want, say Vassily and someone else; they should bring with them some necessities for me and for J. In Perm they can make enquiries at the local Soviet.

Everything has happened so unexpectedly. If you find that the journey to Perm with the children is too far, it would be better, in that case, for you to go to Moscow. They promise that I will be at liberty in Perm. Don't be disheartened, my dearest – God will help us to bear this dreadful ordeal. Give all the Putyatins and everyone else my cordial regards, also to Snegurochka and B.Y. I kiss and embrace you most tenderly – Your Misha.

A little while before Michael's note had arrived, Jack, Natasha's devoted mongrel dog, had suddenly died. He had come into her life at about the same time as she and Michael had fallen in love, and she had come to look on old Jack as a sort of mascot and good-luck charm. He was a symbol of the happy days. Now Jack was dead. She had been sitting quietly by herself, mourning his death, when they brought Michael's note to her. A feeling of terror and doom filled her. What was going to happen now?

11 Perm

One of the first things that Natasha did after the news came of Michael's arrest, was to make some secret arrangements to send George away. She was frightened for his safety; Tata was all right, as she was a Mamontoff – therefore a commoner, but for Georgie it was a different matter entirely. So, as soon as possible, he was sent off to Denmark, accompanied by the governess whose passport had been made out to show her to be the wife of a Danish official travelling with her small son to Denmark.

A telegram arrived from Michael from a place called Vologda (on the way to Perm) dated 14th March 1918:

> Everybody well. Fellow-travellers are nice. Moving extremely slowly by goods train. We don't know when we are going to arrive. It will be quite impossible to travel with children without having a separate car, but taking a direct (passenger) train will be considerably quicker. Must take food for the entire journey. Hoping that Vassily has already left for Perm. Please wire to Perm Post Office poste restante. Kind regards to Znamerovsky and everybody.

This telegram was signed Johnson, the name of Michael's secretary.

As soon as she could, Natasha went to Petrograd to

try to find some news about Michael's release, but all she managed was to obtain permission to go to Perm to visit him, and to stay with him in the hotel where he would be living. Before she could leave for Perm however, there were certain arrangements to be made; firstly Natasha asked a friend of the family, Princess Wiasemsky, to come and live at the house to keep an eye on Tata and the servants; secondly, she arranged for part of the house to be nominally let to some officials of the Danish Embassy. Two young Danes would arrive each morning, and after staying in the house all day, would leave in the evening. As an additional precaution a Danish flag was hung out of a window.

The whole of March passed by before Natasha could finalize all the arrangements and leave for Perm. Meanwhile she and Michael corresponded by letters and telegrams:

Perm 19th March.
Arrived safely. At present are lodging all together in one room. No other accommodation. Vassily not yet arrived. Anxious. This is a second telegram. (This telegram was signed 'Maro'.)

Perm 21st March
Local authorities having so far no instructions have decided to keep us until further notice in solitary confinement in the prison hospital. We have sent telegrams to clear our position to (Commissars) Bruevitch, Lunocharsky and Uritsky. If possible let Dr Cotton and Vera Mikhailovna come here. Vassily has arrived, but was not allowed to see us. Embracing tenderly – Misha.

Perm 26th March.
No reply received to the telegrams of our boss [evidently the Grand Duke]. Everybody lives together in the same conditions. It is very important to the local authorities to

receive directions from Peoples Commissars about granting us freedom. On the direct line by the local Soviet Uritsky gave an evasive reply and leaves the decision to the local Soviet. In view of this everybody will be transferred to the prison hospital. Those visitors wishing to come here should get a special permit. In future please wire me Poste Restante. (This one was signed 'Chely Cheff' which was the name of Michael's valet.)

Perm 6th April.
We shall be probably released on Monday. The doctor arrived yesterday. As soon as lodgings are arranged will wire you. Embracing, your Misha.

Perm 19th April.
Have sent two telegrams in the last ten days. Have received nothing from you and am worrying. It is not practical to rent a flat. We can live in our hotel. Waiting impatiently. Wire me when leaving and how many people. Kissing – Misha.

I have in my possession a letter from Michael to Natasha, and it is dated 28th March 1918 and written from Perm, King's Apartment Rooms.

My very own, dearest Natasha,
At last can I write to you openly, as up to now, i.e., up to last night, we were under arrest and all my correspondence has been checked by the local Soviet. I did not want to write letters, knowing that they would be read by all and sundry. Telegrams were sent by the Post Office to the Soviet. I am sure that at the Post Office there are your telegrams – I do not know how many – I suppose two. I believe you are saying in one of them about Cotton and something else, but I do not know anything about the other one. Today Vassily is going to the Soviet and will request to hand them over to him.
Yesterday morning we were told that we shall be released and we have spent a wearisome day awaiting the

results. Thanks to the insistence of Vassily, we were at last released at 11 pm and went straight away to the rooms we have rented in the King's Apartments. Each of us has his own room, Johnson, Vassily and myself. Cotton, Borunov and Vlassov are in the hotel next door. The poor Znamerovsky has so far not been released and will be transferred to the prison hospital. My head is going round and round – so much I want to tell you as I have lived through so much during the last five weeks since my arrest.

My dearest Natashechka, I thank you with all my heart for the lovely letters and also for all the troubles you have taken to help me. Thank God, the first step was successful, and we are free. This is such a relief already. The second step would be to get away from here and go home, but I'm afraid that this won't be soon. I am terribly lonely without you, my darling – come here as soon as possible. As from today I will start looking for some lodgings for us and as soon as I find something suitable, I will send you a wire.

It would be marvellous if Maria Vassilievna could come with you and stay at least a week. Why should she be in a hurry to leave? Also, invite Snegurochka and Boris Yakovlevich to come here, as they have decided to follow us, when we talked with them in Viatka. Life here will be very dreary, therefore it would be nice to make up a little circle of friends, especially if it is our destiny to be in exile for several months. When at last shall we be able to realize our cherished dream – to go abroad? World events are moving at such a rate and every week brings so much new and unexpected, that perhaps all this is not so far away.

We receive our books from the town library. I will start reading Dostoievsky as soon as Cotton leaves – *Crime and Punishment*. I have recently read an amusing story by the same author, *Uncle's Dream*. I also finished another book, a translation from the French – *Robespierre* What luck that you managed to send me those two books of Markevich. They were a real salvation for me. I read them in the train and afterwards, and in a few days I finished them both.

Cotton will return them to Snegurochka.

There are plenty of foodstuffs here and the prices are two and a half times cheaper than in Petrograd. Mainly there is an abundance of bread, the milk is lovely, butter is good, cream cheese and sour cream are also available.

The weather is spring-like now, high time too! Streams are running in the streets, the sun is shining high in the skies but my heart is melancholy and cheerless. My heart and soul are not here – they were left *there*, where I am loved and constantly thought of, there where can be found those whom I love and who are dear to me. You can rest assured that you continue to take up the greatest part of my heart . . . * *visage adorable* which I have loved so much, and I still want your caresses . . . I think constantly about you, my angel, and it hurts me to think that you have to go through these dreadful times. There is nothing to do but be patient and rely on God.

It is terrible not to be in our dear Gatchina at this lovely time of the year. I was used to spending the spring there and I have so many perfect and delightful memories of my childhood there, and also of the later years. It always seems to me that only there is it really spring. And if you will think of Pushkino, which you loved so much, then you will understand how I feel.

Now, my dear and beloved Natashechka, I will end my letter and hope that you will receive it in about five days. Cotton hopes to leave tomorrow evening by the Express, but if there is none, then he will take the Mail train earlier in the day. It is now my hope to see you here very soon. May God keep you and bless you. I embrace and kiss you tenderly with all my love.

Adoring you, all yours,
Misha.

* In the original letter from Michael to Natasha, there are eleven lines which have been heavily crossed out at this point and are completely illegible. From the context, one would guess that the lines contain references to their intimate life, and I expect that Natasha did not want these to be read by other people.

On the 9th April, Michael and Johnson went for a walk in the town of Perm. They decided to have their photographs taken, and Michael sent the resulting photo to Natasha with the following message written on the reverse side:

> We were photographed during a walk in town, on the Hay Market, where there is a second-hand market. The photo was developed in 10 minutes.
> M.A.
> I have not shaved since we left Gatchina – 22nd Feb.

Just before Natasha was due to leave Petrograd to start her journey to Perm, Michael scribbled a hurried note to her:

> My dear Natashechka.
> A few more words. Please bring me some writing paper, my red seal, a penholder and nibs which we always use; then my blue blotting pad and also the inkstand; (The blotting pad is in the middle drawer of the writing desk;) the folding photo frame with your photographs, the Russian-English-French-German dictionary in one volume, and finally the typewriter – but only if you can carry it and it is not too heavy. I have enough soap, but please bring the large bottle of *White Rose* and also my suppositories, which are on the cupboard in the toilet next to the washstand, and also please bring quite a lot of lavatory paper...

Natasha's journey to Perm took many days but eventually she arrived. She was lucky to manage to book her seat in one of the international carriages on the train as they were far more comfortable that the Russian-type ones. But it was very soon that she had to leave to return to Gatchina; she and Michael were both very concerned as to what was happening there. But before she left, Natasha found a house which she wanted to rent, as she felt that it would be better for Michael than to live in an hotel. Michael missed her very much after her departure and wrote to her:

My dearest Sweetheart, my own darling Natasha, I take the opportunity to send you this letter, first to Moscow, as I think that you are still there. I want to say so much that I do not know how to begin. It is already 16 days since you left. I can't describe how I feel – so depressed and desperate from everything here, from this dreadful town, where I am so upset and am living this pointless life. Why do I write all this when you know it so well yourself?

The question about the flat is dragging on because every day we expect some military action . . . . but so far everything is quiet and therefore D. and I have decided to move, as to continue living here is quite impossible. The price for the flat is rising all the time and the cook gives us enormous bills. I am going tomorrow to see Kobiak's flat which is near the High-School. If I find it suitable, I shall move there as the owners are going away to their summer house. It will be better to live there than in the house which you liked, but where we would have to sit all boxed up, facing a noisy street; whereas here there is more space and we will have a nice view from the balcony which overlooks the river. In the flat in which I am living now there is a dreadful noise day and night, especially towards morning. I am sleeping very badly again, I wake up constantly, probably from sheer boredom. . .

It seems to me that everything is again delayed and we may not be able to see each other for another two months, which would be dreadful, but I so hope that you will be able to come here sooner than that, provided that there is no military coup. It would be better, if you could wait for me to send you a telegram which I hope to be in a position to do soon. I repeat that this would depend entirely on the developments in this region.

My dear soul Natashechka – I do hope that God will allow us to be together again soon, or even better that I will be allowed to return home!

I embrace you and kiss you very tenderly. God bless you.

I am all yours,
Your boy.

P.S. When you come, please bring me Dequequt lotion, some candles, the black Finnish knife, the pair of blue trousers with the turn-ups, and Kodak and the book *The History of the French Revolution* (Miniet).

At the end of May Michael wrote to Natasha a note which he signed 'Correspondent-Observer-On-Tour'. He headed it 'The Recent Political Review':

'I kiss your hand . . . everything here is outwardly calm, but the authorities admit that the moment is rather acute and serious. We have to continue to give our signatures daily in the Committee of 'charms'. In the town squares the railwaymen and party-workers are receiving military training, drill and similar physical exercises; . . . The town is full of rumours and is disturbed by news that in the east, not very far, - in 'Katia's Burg' [Ekaterinburg] there are activities of either Czecho-slovaks or Slovako-czechs. It is rumoured that they have besieged 'Katia' from three sides and even taken Cheliabinsk, thus cutting off Siberia. What their future plans are – nobody knows, but our town is now declared under military law. From yesterday even the clocks are advanced for two hours, so that now, by human standards, everything is in a mess, similar to Shirokoff's turkeys.* *Le Patron† par suite de ces faits étranges et lugubres – tout-a-fait gàgà. Cependant il n'est pas dit que son état normal l'ait complètement abandoné.*

The trains coming from the west are all detained, papers are not arriving regularly but in batches. Whatever is happening is difficult to comprehend. We received papers today which were dated the 29th. Trains from here

---

* Presumably some private joke.
† Was Michael referring to Lenin or to Uritsky?

to the east are only travelling as far as 90 versts. We shall hope that all the storms will by-pass our dear town.

22nd May this letter today. Just received from you your fifth telegram from M. I await the promised letter and parcel impatiently . . . Be careful – all telegrams and letters I receive are opened by the Extreme Comittee. Shall be pleased to hear that you are home again, and very, very much hope that we shall meet again very soon, my dearest Natashechka. All my thoughts are always with you. May God be with you. Tenderly embracing you,

                                      all yours . . .

At the beginning of June Natasha managed to visit Perm again, but she could not stay long. She wanted to return to Gatchina to be with Tata for her birthday on June 15th. She left with her luggage full of presents for her daughter, with a cake and lots of provisions, as food was more plentiful at Perm than at Gatchina.

12 Prison and Freedom

Back at Gatchina, things were not going too well. While Natasha had been visiting Michael in Perm this last time, the local Commissar called Seroff had paid a surprise visit to the house, and had been received by a rather panic-struck Princess Wiasemsky and a frankly very interested fifteen-year-old Tata. He had come to requisition food which was by now in short supply in the town. The news of this visit by a Bolshevik Commissar to the house of a Grand Duke soon made its way to Petrograd, and from that moment on, they were left completely alone; it was as if they had never had any friends at all.

Tata and Princess Wiasemsky were delighted to see Natasha when she returned for Tata's birthday. They were very pleased to see all the provisions that she had brought back with her from Perm, and busied themselves in hiding it all away so that any further visits from Seroff would find them better prepared. Tata enjoyed her birthday, in spite of everything, and though they all missed Michael and Georgie, they managed to have a gay evening. The next day, as Natasha was beginning to make her preparations for her return to Perm, a telegram arrived from a friend there:

Our friend and Johnny have vanished without trace. . .

It was obvious that 'Johnny' referred to Johnson. Natasha immediately left for Petrograd and stormed into the Cheka demanding an interview with Uritsky. It was a violent one; she insisted on knowing what had happened to Michael, and she shouted and raged when told that no one at the Cheka knew anything definite either. Uritsky finally lost his temper too; he told her that he suspected that she was the one who knew perfectly well where Michael was, and that she had been personally involved in his disappearance; so he had no alternative than to imprison her until she was prepared to tell him the truth. So Natasha, still shouting, was taken upstairs to the women's prison, Gorokhovaya No. 2. Natasha's friend, Mme Abakanovitch, who had accompanied her to the Cheka, insisted on being imprisoned as well.

The two women then proceeded to make the best of things, and were determined to make their enforced imprisonment as pleasant as possible. Mme Abakanovitch sent a message to her house in Petrograd which included a long list of items she desired to be sent forthwith to the prison. It was not long before a stream of servants arrived at the Cheka with luggage, beds, bedding, linen, crockery, books, candles, cushions, towels and food. Very soon the two women had made themselves comfortable. They hung sheets on the walls to cover up the dirty paintwork, and they placed gaily coloured cushions wherever possible until their cell resembled a ladies' boudoir. Each day the maid from the Abakanovitch house would bring in freshly cooked food for them to eat. Natasha was the bane of the Cheka; she never stopped demanding this, complaining of that, and she treated everyone as half-witted serfs with whom she was obliged to deal through no fault of her own.

One day special permission was obtained for Tata to visit her mother in the Cheka, but she took with her only bad news. Seroff had got into the habit of paying frequent surprise visits to the house at Gatchina, and was more and more rude and unpleasant each time. Still none of their erstwhile friends came to see them any more. There was no news at all about Michael. When Tata had to leave to return home, she promised to come and see Natasha again as soon as possible.

In July they heard the news of the massacre of the Tsar and his family at Ekaterinburg. No one believed it could possibly be true and put it down to a piece of Bolshevik propaganda.*

After ten months in prison, Natasha was moved to a nursing home. She had been pretending to be ill for some time, and had been coughing pathetically and had complained of a frequent pain in her chest. The prison doctor must have realized that she was only feigning, but nevertheless diagnosed the trouble as tuberculosis. Tata was given special permission to visit Natasha in the Nursing Home and found her in bed to keep up appearances, but in actual fact looking very pale and tired. They discussed their plans to escape. It was agreed that they would try to travel separately to Kiev where they would meet up at the house of some good friends. So Tata said good bye to her mother and returned to Gatchina to get ready for her flight. That same night Natasha calmly arose from her bed and walked out unobserved from the Nursing Home. Before Tata could

* See Appendix.

leave the next morning, Seroff came storming in and demanded to know where Natasha was and insisted on searching the house. Tata was rather rude to him and provoked him, and so in his fury he arrested her for complicity in her mother's escape, and she was taken to the Cheka and locked up in the very room in which her mother had been held. One of the women there said that she remembered Natasha very well, and how marvellous it was to see how she had had everyone running around executing her orders at the double, and she added with a sigh that it was quite different now. By this time Uritsky had been shot by a Jewish student, and since then things had changed for the worse at the prison and the discipline had become much more severe.

After four days of interrogation Tata was freed. She had no money on her at all, so she thought it would be best to walk to her uncle Matveiev's flat and ask him for help to return to Gatchina. But there was no answer at the door of the flat, and Tata just sat down and cried. Suddenly Natasha and Princess Wiasemsky came down from the flat upstairs where they had been hiding, judging that the safest place for them to hide was in the same building that their relation lived; thus they could keep an eye on the comings and goings of the hunters. Princess Wiasemsky was wearing a bright red wig which she thought to be a good disguise. Tata was taken to the flat upstairs and immediately given a bath and had her hair washed; after her stay at the Cheka she was covered with vermin. Then they held a Council of War. It was decided that Tata should return to Gatchina as if nothing had happened after her release from the Cheka, should collect her passport and leave as soon as possible. A close woman friend, Mme Yachontoff, was all ready and would accompany Tata to Kiev. this would not be too difficult as Tata had her own passport in her real name of Mamontoff; most people had forgotten that this was her real name. Princess Wiasemsky was alright too, as she had her passport, but Natasha would have to wait in hiding while some friends provided one for her in a false name. So they made their plans to meet at Kiev, and then Tata left the flat and returned to Gatchina.

Eventually the kind friends managed to obtain Natasha's false passport, and she left Petrograd for Kiev wearing the uniform of a Red Cross nurse which they had managed to find. The train left from the Nicholaevsky station which was packed with people carrying bundles of bedding, kitchen utensils and battered suitcases. Everyone was shouting and pushing as they tried to clamber aboard the already crowded train. As the friends had reserved a seat for her, she did not have too much trouble in boarding the train. She immediately sat down and tried to keep out of sight in case any of the Cheka Officials were around. By now she was feeling far from well; the experiences of the last few months were telling on her; she had a bad cough, a pain in her side, a bad headache, and had constant spells of shivering. After a long wait the train finally moved off. Natasha, as she looked out of the windows, said a mental goodbye to St Petersburg; perhaps for ever, perhaps just for a while, who could know?... She sat back and closed her eyes and tried to sleep as the train puffed its way slowly along.

When they arrived at Orcha, the Bolshevik frontier with the Ukraine, everyone was made to get out of the train. The waiting-rooms were crammed with people, whole families were camped out on the platforms, cooking on spirit-stoves, suckling their babies, screaming at their children while dogs ran barking everywhere. Everyone was waiting for their permits to leave Bolshevik Russia, and once those were obtained, they had to wait for other permits to enter the Ukraine, which at that time was under German jurisdiction. Natasha's heart missed a beat when she saw everyone's luggage being taken to a shed to be examined; her cases contained some of her fabulous fur coats and quite a lot of jewellery. But she tried to appear unconcerned as she followed her luggage into the shed, and just hoped that no one would recognize her. Perhaps it was because she was wearing the Red Cross Nurse's uniform, but no one paid any special attention to her, and her cases were merely opened, prodded, and then re-shut. She was free to walk a couple of hundred yards to the German frontier post. There was no trouble there, and she was allowed to enter the Ukraine. As soon as she could, she boarded another train to take her south to Kiev. This train was crowded, but it was not as bad as the one from Petrograd. She had bought a lot of food before leaving Orcha; bread, butter, cold meats, cream cheese and bottles of *kvass*, but she was still feeling ill and was not hungry, only thirsty. When the train stopped at various villages, the peasants would crowd round the train selling apples, pears, plums and watermelons, and Natasha bought some fruit and felt refreshed after eating some.

After a day's travelling, she changed trains at Gomel and was lucky to find a vacant sleeping-berth. She slept fitfully that night, and reached Kiev at lunch time. She had telegraphed her time of arrival from Gomel, and Tata and Princess Wiasemsky were at the station to meet her. When they arrived at the house of their friends, who were called Davidoff, Natasha went straight to bed, and a doctor was called. He diagnosed pleurisy, and she was quite ill for a while. The Davidoffs were very kind and looked after her very well, and by the time she recovered, she decided that they should leave for Odessa – they could not possibly trespass on the kindness of the Davidoffs any longer. So they said their goodbyes to their friends, and made plans to meet up in London, as the Davidoffs intended going to England as well as soon as they could. So Natasha, Tata and Princess Wiasemsky went to Odessa and stayed at the Hôtel de Londres. They had plenty of money as Tata had managed to smuggle out some furs and jewellery as well from Russia; Natasha's fabulous pearl ear-rings, each pearl the size of a hazelnut, had been hidden in an innocent-looking tablet of soap, so they felt that they did not have to worry about finances. Odessa was full of wild rumours – it was said that Kiev had fallen to the Bolsheviks and was the scene of dreadful massacres; the Reds were said to be marching on Odessa and the Crimea. Natasha went to the Rumanian Consulate to try to get permits to go to Rumania, but learned with horror that they were too late; Rumania had closed her frontiers to any more Russian refugees. So what was going to happen to them, where could they go? Natasha spent a sleepless night worrying, but the next morning came news of the Armistice, and their spirits rose. Surely the Allied Fleets would soon arrive at Odessa, and someone would help them, know what to do. The first ship to arrive was a French battleship; the French came and policed the town and restored order efficiently, but there was no talk of evacuating women and children at all. The French authorities, when approached about this, were most evasive. Then one day the (British) Royal Navy arrived, in the form of *HMS Nereide*. Natasha, Tata and Princess Wiasemsky rushed down to the harbour, and Tata was sent on board to ask permission for her mother and friends to come aboard. All three women were immediately invited to take tea in the wardroom. So overjoyed were they at the prospect of safety at long last that they laughed and chattered gaily with the officers and treated them as dear friends and saviours. The officers not unaturally were somewhat taken aback and at the same time pleasantly surprised at this warmth and friendliness from three women whom they had never seen before. The logical conclusion was that they were ladies of easy virtue from Odessa, and it was not long before Natasha found an enthusiastic arm encircling her waist. She hurriedly begged Tata, who spoke the most fluent English, to explain the true circumstances as quickly as possible, and this Tata did. Profuse apologies followed, and much laughter, and to show that there were no hard feelings, Natasha invited the officers to take tea at the hotel the next afternoon. This set the pattern for the next few days; one day they would all go on board the *Nereide* for refreshments; the next day the officers would go to the Hôtel de Londres. Meanwhile signals were being sent to the Admiralty for permission to transport these three women away from Odessa to a place of safety. Odessa started to come under shell-fire as the Red Army approached nearer and nearer, and one of the officers gave Natasha a small pistol to use in emergencies, but she was so frightened of it that she locked it away in one of her cases. By now, *Nereide* had been joined by *HMS Skirmisher*, and one night, when the sound of gunfire seemed especially near, the three women were taken on board *Skirmisher* to spend the night as a precaution. It was said at the time that they were the first women officially allowed to spend the night on a British man-of-war since Lady Hamilton. The next day permission arrived from the Admiralty and the women were transferred to *Nereide* for passage to Constantinople.

On arrival at Constantinople they booked rooms at the Pera Palace Hotel, and Natasha started to make enquiries from everyone as to whether there was any news of Michael, but no one knew anything definite. There were all sorts of rumours, and Natasha did not know what to believe. By then there were already many Russians at Constantinople who had fled Russia, and Natasha was so pleased to find many old friends among them. They all recounted their stories of their flight and escape, but not one knew anything definite about Michael. Natasha had so hoped to hear news of his safety on her arrival at Constantinople; she had even sometimes hoped to actually find him there, waiting for her. Her friends, to distract her, insisted on her joining them for picnics and sightseeing tours, and invited her to dinner parties. A whole month passed by in this way, and then permission was obtained from the Admiralty again for them to be conveyed, this time to Malta, on board *HMS Agamemnon*, which was returning to Chatham to pay off.

The Captain, Captain Litchfield-Speer, gave up his own quarters for the passengers, and they left for Malta.

Natasha hoped that there would be some news to be had of Michael when they arrived there. The Captain was very sympathetic when he heard their story, and did all he could to reassure Natasha; he organized dinner parties and entertainments to help pass the journey. Lord Methuen, then Governor of Malta, began to send what seemed strange wireless messages addressed to Natasha, insisting that she stay at Government House on her arrival at Malta. Natasha begged to be excused in her replies, saying that she would prefer to stay at an hotel. The answers to this could only be taken to mean 'Nonsense, Old Girl!' It eventually turned out that Lord Methuen had thought that Lady Brassey, an old friend of his, was on board, and had not realized that it was in fact the Countess Brassow. On the fourth day they arrived at Valetta, and they took a suite at the Osborne Hotel. But no one had heard any definite news at all about Michael's whereabouts. They stayed at Malta for a few weeks, hoping every day for news. To pass the time they accepted invitations to lunch-parties, dinner-parties, receptions at Government House, and even once went to the opera. Natasha decided that she wanted to leave for England, and hoped that there would be good news for them either on the way, in France, or at least on arrival in London. They boarded the *Isonzo*, a merchant ship, and after a couple of days, arrived at Marseille. No one there knew anything at all about Michael. From Marseille they went by train to Paris; nothing. Rumours were plentiful, but still there was nothing definite. To console herself Natasha went on a shopping-spree and bought herself and Tata lots of new dresses and hats. Then from England came word that Michael's property there had been transferred from Frant, near Tunbridge Wells to Wadhurst in Sussex, and that Mme Johnson, the mother of Michael's secretary, was already in residence in charge of a few servants, awaiting Natasha's arrival. Tata was sent off to a convent school in France; and then Natasha and Princess Wiasemsky went to the house, which was called Snape, and waited for each day to bring news that Michael and Johnson were safe; but this news never came.

PART THREE
SURVIVAL

13 Aftermath

Every day, on rising in the morning, Natasha would say to Mme Johnson, 'I am sure we will have good news today' and she would produce a reason for her hopes: 'I saw two magpies flying together this morning,' or 'A black cat sat in the garden and stared at me for three minutes.' The Russians are a very superstitious race, and though it was the country people who paid the greatest attention to omens of this sort, Natasha had by this time come to put her faith into such signs as well. If she broke a fingernail on a Sunday, and was obliged to trim it with her scissors, she was in the depth of despair, for was it not unlucky to cut one's nails on a Sunday? If, on the other hand, there was a favourable sign, such as a magpie flying across her path closely followed by its mate, and if she remembered to knock on wood and blow them a kiss, then all would be well and she would rush to find Mme Johnson to tell her. The two women would weep and exclaim, and pour themselves out a small glass of liqueur to help them recapture their composure, and to drink a toast to the happy days of reunion with their loved ones, which according to the happy omen, would be very soon.

But sometimes Natasha would wake at night from her light sleep, and lie in bed weeping until dawn. For it was at these times that she would lose all hope of ever seeing Michael again. But come morning, she would manage to greet Mme Johnson with a smile and to whisper to her: 'I am sure it will be to-day . . .' and when evening came and there had been no news, she would say 'Well . . . there is always to-morrow' and smile cheerfully, while in her heart despair was growing.

It was to be almost fifteen years before Natasha knew for certain* what had happened to her darling Misha. In 1934, a book caled *The Last Days of Tsardom* by P.M. Bykov, sometime Chairman of the Ekaterinburg Soviet, was published, and in it was the following account:

> Since March 1917 he [Michael] had lived with his family at Gatchina. Only a year later, in February 1918, owing to the monarchist movement in his favour, he was arrested on the demand of the Petrograd Soviet and sent with his secretary N. Johnson, to Perm. The accompanying letter to the Perm Soviet stated that Michael Romanov was being sent to Perm on the responsibility and under the observation of the Soviet, but it suggested that no special restrictions be imposed upon him. . . . Reckoning with the danger of allowing Michael to live freely in Perm, and with the possibility of irresponsible acts, the Perm Soviet suggested to him that he should be transferred to a specially fitted-up section of the prison hospital. Romanov made a complaint to the Council of People's Commissaries and the All-Russian Extraordinary Commission. In reply to this complaint, the Perm Soviet received an instruction . . . to liberate Michael Romanov but retain him under observation, and another letter . . . signed by Uritsky, granting Romanov the right of free sojourn in Perm . . . and that the Soviet did not take responsibility for anything that might happen.

* See Appendix.

Romanov and his secretary Johnson, his valet Chelyshev and his chauffeur Borunov settled down in the Sibirskaya Ulitsa, – one of the busiest streets in Perm – in the King's Hotel, the best in town, near the river Kama. . . . Meanwhile, influenced by the demands of the Perm and Motovilikha workers for the execution of Michael Romanov, a secret group was formed with the object of killing him. . . . The group had no connection with either Party or Soviet organisations, and acted in great secret at its own risk.

On the evening of June 12–13 this group came to the hotel with forged documents from the Provisional Extraordinary Commission. Michael Romanov was already asleep. He was awakened and presented with a document ordering him immediately to leave Perm. Romanov was incredulous, and refused to follow his visitors, demanding that they should call a doctor and Malkov, chairman of the Extraordinary Commission. They then said that they would use force. The ex-Grand Duke's secretary Johnson said that he would follow his 'master'. Although Johnson did not enter into the plans of the group, they decided however to take him along in order not to delay in the hotel. Both the 'arrested' men were put into carriages which were ready, and taken out of the town along the track to Motovilikha. After passing the Nobel kerosine dump, six versts from Motovilikha, they turned off into the forest to the right and there shot Michael Romanov.* After this, in order to cover up their tracks, one of those participating rang up the militia and the Provisional Extraordinary Commission and informed them that some persons unknown had entered the King's hotel the previous night and had carried off Michael Romanov in the direction of Siberia.

This event was a complete surprise for all organisations of Perm. A chase was organised immediately which however set out on the false route and could find no traces. At the same time telegrams were sent to Petrograd and in every

---

* and Johnson as well.

direction announcing the escape of Michael Romanov. . . .

So at last, in 1934 only, Natasha read these words and knew what had happened to her Misha, the last of the Romanoff Tsars of Imperial Russia, whose 'reign' must be the shortest on record. But what about the other people whose names appear in this story about one of the most fascinating periods of history – what happened to them?

Michael and Nicholas had seen each other just before the former was taken away to Perm, and just before Nicholas was sent by Kerensky to Tobolsk. Michael wrote in his diary for 31st July 1917:

> At 12 noon the Palace Commandant arrived and we went together to the Alexander Palace. We entered the Palace from the kitchen side and then went through the cellar and passed to the fourth entrance to Nicky's reception room, where we found Count Benkendorff, Kerensky, V. Dolgoruki and two young officers. From there I went through to Nicky's study where I met Nicky in the presence of Kerensky and a duty officer. I found Nicky looking quite well; I stayed with him for 10 minutes and then I left and returned to Boris (the Grand Duke Boris Vladimirovitch) and later went back to Gatchina. This meeting with Nicky was arranged by Kerensky, and I found out later that Nicky and his family were leaving that same night for Tobolsk.

What Michael did not write was that according to the account of this meeting by Count Benkendorff, he (Michael) left this meeting in tears.

The forced journey made by Nicholas and his family to Tobolsk and eventually on to Ekaterinburg is too well-known to bear repetition, and how the steamer on which they travelled from Tyumen to Tobolsk, passed by Pokrovskoe, the birth-place of Rasputin who had predicted that they would one day visit his village. The massacre of Nicholas and his wife, children and servants has been described over and over again, and everyone knows the terrible details of how, after their execution, their bodies were taken on a truck to a lonely piece of land, chopped into bits, burned, dissolved in acid, and how the residue was thrown into a dis-used mine shaft.*

Michael's mother, the Dowager Empress Marie, left Russia in April 1919 on board *HMS Marlborough*. All during the voyage to England she was very gay and happy and confided to some people that she had had secret information that her son Nicholas and his wife and family had escaped from Ekaterinburg, and that they were safe.† She stayed for a while in England, and then went to Denmark where she lived in a wing of the Royal Palace of her nephew, King Christian X. She had managed to take her jewels out of Russia with her, and she kept them in a large box under her bed. Marie and her nephew did not try to disguise the fact that they disliked each other very much, and they spent a great deal of the time arguing about money matters and petty details concerning the amount of electricity consumed by the Dowager Empress in her own apartments. King Christian kept on hinting that she should sell some of her jewels to help to pay for her keep, but she steadfastly refused. She died in Copenhagen in 1928 at the age of eighty-one, five years before the publication of Paul Bykov's book, *The Last Days of Tsardom*, in which the

* See Appendix.
† See Appendix.

massacre at Ekaterinburg was described, and in which Michael's murder was admitted to as well. She had always refused to believe the reports about Ekaterinburg, and she had never let herself give up hope that her Misha had survived safe and sound too. So it is nice to know that she was spared the dreadful truth.*

As for Olga, she left Russia with her husband, Captain Koulikovsky, and their two small sons. They sailed from the Crimea to Constantinople on board a merchant ship. They were interned for two or three weeks on one of the beautiful islands in the Sea of Marmora called Prinkipo or Büyükada, as it is now called. From there they went to Belgrade and then on to Copenhagen where her mother, the Dowager Empress Marie, was living her last days. Marie was worrying about her jewel box and became convinced that everyone was after it, so she had it moved from under her bed to a place in her room where she could actually see it while lying in bed, for she was bed-ridden by now, and was very ill. Olga looked after her mother devotedly during this period, and Xenia used to come over from England, where she had settled, to visit her. On many of these occasions Marie would talk about her jewels, how the contents of the box would one day belong to her two daughters. 'You will have all of it when I am gone' she said to them again and again.† King Christian almost overtly suggested that he expected to receive a good share from the eventual sale of the jewels to recompense him for his kindness and expenses to his aunt in the past. George V wrote to his 'dear Aunt Minnie' suggesting that she should arrange for the jewels to be deposited in

* See Appendix.
† *The Last Grand Duchess*, Ian Vorres.

a bank in London for safe-keeping, and that he would personally see to the arrangements for their sale, if she so wished. Grand Duke Alexander, Xenia's estranged husband, wrote from France that she should at least pawn the jewels to enable the exiled Romanoffs to open a paper factory so that they could all live decently on the revenue. 'Dear Aunt Minnie' had the box brought even nearer to her bed and refused to let it out of her sight for a moment. Eventually, after being in a coma for three days and three nights, Marie died. As soon as the funeral was over. Xenia left to return to London, taking the jewel box with her as George V had suggested. Olga, it seems, was so innocent and unwordly that she did not even wonder why there was such a hurry to get this box to England. Xenia had told her that as she (Olga) had a commoner for a husband, the whole business did not concern her. Olga merely felt grateful to 'uncle Georgie' that he had been so concerned over its safety. A few days after the funeral King Christian called on Olga and asker her what had happened to the jewel box. She was rather surprised, but answered him that it was on its way to London at the suggestion of George V. King Christian was furious.

In his memoirs Sir Frederick Ponsonby mentions that he had been instructed by King George V to have the jewels taken to England for safety. They were taken to Buckingham Palace and Xenia and Sir Frederick were present when the box was opened:

> ... Ropes of the most wonderful pearls were taken out, all graduated, the largest being the size of a big cherry. ... Cabuchon emeralds and large rubies and sapphires were laid out. ...

The jewellery was valued by Hennel & Sons, and they

were prepared to make an immediate advance of £100,000 on the contents of the box, and in fact eventually their sale made £350,000. But there is a mystery – Xenia received £60,000 as her share, and Olga received £40,000 making the grand total of £100,000. Where did the extra £250,000 go? Olga wrote later in her memoirs:

> Yes, indeed, there are certain aspects in this affair which I could never understand, and I have tried not to think about it too much, and certainly I've never talked to anyone, except my husband. I know that May (Queen Mary) was passionately fond of fine jewelry. I remember how in 1925 the Soviet Government, being badly in need of foreign currency, sent a lot of Romanoff jewels to be sold in England, and I heard that May had bought quite a few – including a collection of Fabergé's Easter eggs. I also know that at least one item of my own property, looted from the palace in Petrograd, was among the lot shipped to England, but its price proved too high even for May, and I suppose it is still in the Kremlin. It was one of my wedding presents – an exquisite fan made of mother-of-pearl and studded all over with diamonds and pearls. . . .

Soon after the sale some of the more important pieces appeared in Queen Mary's collection, and other people were seen wearing Romanoff jewels too, but the balance of £250,000 was never mentioned at all.

After Marie's death, King Christian of Denmark was so annoyed that the jewels had been taken to London that he became rather unpleasant to Olga and her family, so they moved from the palace at Hvidore to a wealthy Dane's private estate nearby, and Koulikovsky took a job as manager of the stables. Eventually, many years later, they managed to buy a large farm at Ballerup, fifteen miles north-west of Copenhagen. They felt that they had reached a haven, there to spend the rest of their days in peace. But this was not to be. By the end of 1940 the Nazis had overrun the whole of Denmark and life was not so pleasant; when Hitler invaded Russia and Stalin's troops were not so far away, Olga and Koulikovsky decided to make arrangements to be ready to leave Denmark if it became necessary. But they stayed on until after the war was ended when pressure was exerted from the Kremlin for her extradition on a charge of her having helped some Russians to defect. Then she and her husband left Denmark and sailed to Canada as 'Agricultural Immigrants' which meant that they would have to work on a farm there after their arrival. Koulikovsky died in 1958 in Cooksville, nursed devotedly by his wife. In the autumn of 1959 she had lunch with Queen Elizabeth II on board the *Britannia*, and she met Lord and Lady Mountbatten when they visited Canada in August 1959. Then Olga's health began to deteriorate, and she would lie in bed remembering her childhood in faraway Russia.

> At Gatchina in the park there was a little bridge over a cataract. It roared with a deafening noise, and the bridge seemed so fragile that most people were afraid of crossing it. If they did, they would just run, never linger for an instant. Well, my brother Michael and I would often go there and stand on the bridge. It would probably be no more than a few minutes. It always seemed hours to me. We were terribly scared and we shook as we stood looking at the thundering foaming water below. But it was well worth it every time. We left the bridge excited and conscious that we had achieved something. I wanted you to know about that little bridge because I am going to die with the same sense of achievement. However little I had to give, I don't think I withheld anything to serve my dear country as a Romanoff. . . .*

* *The Last Grand Duchess*, by Ian Vorres, Hutchinson 1964.

Olga was moved to Toronto General Hospital and was too ill to be given the telegram which arrived from England announcing the death of her sister Xenia in April 1960. Olga died on 24th November 1960.

Prince Youssoupoff settled in Paris in 1920 and during the years wrote several books about his experiences in Russia before and during the revolution. His generosity to poverty-stricken exiled compatriots was well-known. He and his wife became involved in numerous law suits arising from films and stories of the assassination of Rasputin. Some they won; others they lost. He died on 27th September 1967 aged eighty.

Lenin died on 21st January 1924 near Moscow, after a series of strokes. Trotsky wrote the following testimonial:

> ... Lenin's outward appearance was distinguished by simplicity and strength. He was below middle height, with plebeian features of the Slavonic type of face, brightened by piercing eyes; and his powerful forehead and still more powerful head gave him a marked distinction. He was tireless in work to an unparalleled degree. He put the same exemplary conscientiousness into reading lectures in a small workmen's club in Zurich as into organising the first Socialist State in the world. ...

Kerensky fled to England; he later went to France, and in 1940 moved to the United States of America to live. He wrote many books about the revolution and the murder of the Romanoffs. In his book *The Crucifixion of Liberty,* which was published in New York in 1934, he commented on the fact that both Lenin and he were children of Siberia:

> Let no one say that Lenin is an expression of some kind of

allegedly Asiatic 'elemental' force. I was born under the same sky, I breathed the same air, I heard the same peasant songs and played in the same college playground. I saw the same limitless horizons from the same high bank of the Volga, and I know in my blood and bones . . . that it is only by losing all touch with our native land, only by stamping out all native feeling for it, only so could one do what Lenin did in deliberately and cruelly mutilating Russia.

Kerensky died in New York as recently as 11th June 1970.

Rodzyanko died in 1924 in Belgrade, blamed to the end by the White Russians for the overthrow of the Romanoffs.

Maurice Paléologue returned to Paris and became a senior official in the French Ministry for Foreign Affairs. He was elected a member of the *Académie Française*. He died in Paris in 1944 during the liberation of the city, and was buried in the cemetery at Passy.

The Grand Duke Nicholas Mikhailovitch, letter-writer extraordinary, was arrested in Vologda on 1st July 1918 together with his brother George and Grand Duke Dimitri Constantinovitch on the orders of Uritsky himself. They were taken to Petrograd and thrown into a prison dungeon where they remained for six months. A French journalist called Paul Erio, who was Special Correspondent for a French newspaper and who was based in Helsinki, sent the following report to Paris:

> Wakened and taken from his cell during the night of 27–28th January 1919, the Grand Duke Nicholas Mikhailovitch thought that he was being taken to Moscow; he did not think for one minute that he was being taken to his execution and so he took a kitten with him in his arms which he had looked after in prison. He got into the back of a lorry with his brother George and Grand Duke Dimitri

Constantinovitch and four convicts. It was 1.20 when the lorry finally left escorted by six Red Guards.

They were driven to the Fortress of Peter and Paul where they were joined by the Grand Duke Paul whom they hardly recognized as he had lost so much weight. They got out of the lorry and were roughly pushed towards the execution area. A large trench had been dug in the earth there, making a black stain on the white snow.

When the Grand Dukes were lined up in front of the trench the Platoon Commander ordered them to take off their fur coats and jackets.

At that moment the Grand Duke Nicholas began to speak. What did he say? I was unable to find out exactly. He spoke at length, I was told, and his calm demeanour in the face of death made a profound impression on even the Red Guards.

Then the four Grand Dukes embraced each other. Nicholas gave his kitten a last kiss and handed it to a soldier. The poor men then undressed. They were all killed by the same salvo of fire. Then the bodies, stripped of their clothing, were thrown into the gaping trench behind.

Sergei Mamontoff, Natasha's first husband, lived in Estonia and worked with the State Opera at Tallinn. He must have been a courageous man, for he married again and had several more children. But this time he chose as his wife a woman called Pauline, who was decidedly no beauty and was rather plain. Mamontoff wrote to his nephew in Paris, '. . . I can assure you that no Grand Duke is going to look at this one!'

He died in Tallinn in 1938.

14 Exile—England

The England that Natasha found when she arrived in 1919 was a different place from the England she had left in 1914. The wave of change had already started to be felt before the war, but hostilities had put a stop to it, while the country got down to the serious business of fighting. For while Russia had been boiling up for a political revolution, England had been feeling similar stirrings, but these had been spiritual and artistic rather than purely political. Women's suffrage had become law at the end of 1918, the old exclusive 'Society' had been invaded by people of great wealth rather than of good breeding; there was cubism in painting, new conventions in sculpture; new music and new writing; in literature George Bernard Shaw, H. G. Wells and Galsworthy were preaching new and disturbing gospels, and women's skirts were becoming shorter and shorter.

The 18th January 1919 saw the first session of the Conference of Versailles to try to sort out the mess which had been left by the war, and the Prime Minister, Lloyd George, attended it accompanied by Balfour, Bonar Law and G. N. Barnes. While they were out of the country, the miners' long-held grievances resulted in strikes, and a Royal Commission was appointed in

February to issue an interim report on the situation as quickly as possible. The great plans for a gradual demobilization were unsuccessful and there were serious troubles in the demobilization camps as the men returned from the war, and in the end demobilization had to be carried out wholesale thus increasing the already serious problems of unemployment. The situation in Ireland deteriorated rapidly; there was a question of having two parliaments, one for Ulster, and the other for the rest of Ireland with a single council to bring harmony. The *Sinn Fein* refused to accept partition and wanted an independent Irish Republic. The Government reinforced the Irish constabulary with ex-servicemen who had no police training or police traditions, and they acquired notoriety as the 'Black and Tans'. There was a long sad story of ambushings, killings, raids, violent street fighting in Dublin and Belfast, and one comes to the sad conclusion that it does not seem so very different nowadays.

In 1919 the railway workers went on strike for nine days for higher wages; in 1920 the miners went on strike.

On the continent, France, as a reparation for war, intended to occupy Germany's industrial heartland, the Ruhr. They expected the active co-operation of Great Britain in this, but the British Government mistrusted the motives of the French, and would not agree to this step. The French were angry and called this negative attitude a 'betrayal of the Alliance'.

In Russia, things had been happening since Natasha had made her way to Kiev in the uniform of a Red Cross nurse, and had boarded *HMS Nereide* and then *HMS Agamenon* to take her to safety. Lenin had not had it all his own way; small British forces had landed at Murmansk and Archangel, and the Bolsheviks declared that a state of war existed between Russia and her former allies. About one hundred thousand Czech troops began to fight the Bolsheviks on their way to Vladivostok; British, French, Japanese and even U.S. troops supported the counter-revolutionary forces of Admiral Alexander Kolchak who had succeeded in temporarily overthrowing Bolshevism in Eastern Russia. Admiral Kolchak assumed the title of 'Supreme Ruler of Russia' on 18th November 1918, and set up the Headquarters of the 'Russian Government' at Omsk. After some successes in the first half of 1919, the anti-Bolshevik army disintegrated, and the capital of the Russian Government of Omsk was captured by the Bolsheviks in November 1919. Admiral Kolchak resigned and designated General Denikin as his successor. Kolchak was shot by the Bolsheviks at Irkutsk in 1920. Denikin managed to escape to England and settled for a time at Eastbourne. By the end of the war, the Allies were in a position to destroy the Bolshevik regime – but the German retreat imposed on them by the Armistice enabled the Bolsheviks to equip themselves with abandoned German weapons and turn the tables on the White Russians who were eventually left to sink by the war-weary and vacillating Allies. On top of this, a terrible famine ravished Russia, and the Western Powers, in a wave of humanitarian feeling had sent aid to the famished population; thereby they not only saved millions of starving people, but also consolidated the power of the Bolsheviks.

Natasha tried to settle down at Snape. It is obvious from her letters at the time to Captain Litchfield-Speer that she was very lonely and unhappy, and felt lost all by herself without her husband. It helped her to write to the captain, and she looked forward to receiving his letters:

> ... Could I think when I saw you for the first time at Pera Palace, and was too shy of my bad English, that we will become such great friends (as you are for me also a dearly loved friend) and that because of your friendship I do not feel so alone in this strange country. ...
>
> ... I don't know how to thank you for such nice and kind letters, you are such a dear. ...

The Litchfield-Speers and Natasha saw quite a lot of one another during 1919:

> ... Only a few words to thank you for your kind hospitality. It was so very kind of you to think of me and give me so much pleasure. You know how much I enjoy everything to do with the Navy, and especially with you. ...
>
> ... Just a few words to thank you for the nice day I spent with you yesterday. You must know how I am happy to be with you, so that everything that I can explain in my bad English will never be enough! So full stop!! ... with my love to you *always* dearest Captain, your old friend, N. Brassow.

George arrived from Denmark. She wrote to her friend the captain:

> It is already a fortnight that my little son is with me. He is getting a young rascal and wants a strong hand to manage him, but it is really nice to have him with me again and the house seems not to be so empty!

But it was soon time to think of George's education:

> ... I am going with Mr M. and Georgie to St Leonards-on-Sea College to present him to the school where he is entering on the 22nd September.

After Georgie went off to school, she was alone again:

> I am quite alone now with Mme G. as both Tata and Georgie left for their schools. Georgie is very miserable and home-sick and always asking to come back to me. I miss him *dreadfully* as he is my only love at present!

She wrote very often to Georgie. One of her letters to him began:

> ... I have not written to you for three whole days, but that does not mean that I have not been thinking of you all the time, my darling....

It was not a very bad school, probably rather better than most others of its kind. It looked like a private house at first sight, set in a large garden full of flower beds, and approached by a wooded drive. There was also a paddock where the boys were allowed to keep rabbits. There were about sixty pupils, and as long as a boy was good at games and was not too much of a dunce to be able to learn simple lessons, his life was bearable. But for the two other Russian boys there with George, it was different. They were too strange, too unlike the other boys in their manners, customs and temperament, so that they were teased unmercifully most of the time. George had a strong temper, inherited no doubt from his Mamma, and was easily roused to a fury. The fact that, during the winter months he had also to bear the painful irritation of bad chilblains did nothing to help him control it. A bout of teasing him invariably ended in a fight in which George always came out the loser, in tears, with broken chilblains.

One day Natasha went down to St Leonards to take George out to tea, and took also a young fellow-pupil as George's guest. He was named Gore, and is now the Earl of Arran, who kindly wrote to me to tell me his memories of that tea-party.

> ... I remember her as a lady of immense beauty and dignity, which is strange, for little boys don't notice these things much generally – and I also remember that she put jam in my tea. This apparently, and as she told me at the time, is a Russian Custom. ... I do recall, however, that she was wearing a white turban sort of hat which showed up her skin and her long neck to perfection. I also seem to remember that she wore pearls. The tea-party was at Eversfield Hotel which was in those days the smart hotel in St Leonards. ...

In July 1919 she was summoned to London to meet the Dowager Empress Marie. This would be the first time that the two women had ever met face to face. She wrote to her 'dear Captain':

> ... and I have again to go to London with Georgie tomorrow morning, as the Empress wants to see us. It will be a very *pénible* interview, so I am quite upset and even getting ill at the thought of meeting!

After it was over she sent Captain Litchfield-Speer this account of the meeting:

> The interview with the Empress was not too *pénible* as I thought it would be. She was rather nice to me, but I feel that she does not like me and will never forgive me that I married her son. ... She told me that I have very much grown since she saw me the last time (10 years ago) and have changed so much that she would never recognise me.

I could not ask her, was it for the best or for the worse, but afterwards Mme Johnson who went to see all of them at Marlborough House on Wednesday told me that the Empress repeated several times about me: '*Quelle belle femme, comme elle est jolie, je n'en reviens pas.*' I can tell you that because you know me enough to know that I am *very* modest and not at all of that opinion. Queen Alexandra and Princess Victoria were also present and very charming with Georgie and me. We stayed about one hour and then went to lunch with the Grand Duchess Xenia at her flat in Draycott Place.

Meanwhile, in March 1919 Tata had written secretly to Captain Litchfield-Speer:

... The fact is that we have received very bad news about my step-father, they say he has been caught somewhere in the Ural mountains and has been murdered on the spot. Ghastly details are also given. Mother knows nothing about this. It may not be true, so why give her pain without need? The Princess (Wiasemsky) is trying to find out all about it, she is sending letters to everybody she can think of that might know something....

But the news reached Natasha, and in August that year she wrote to the captain:

... I am feeling quite rotten all these days, because although I had two good news of my husband from Russia, I had one very bad from Colonel Davidson. He wrote to Mme Johnson that there is no more hope that my husband and her son are alive. I feel it is true, all the time goes and still we have no news! It becomes for me a real *open wound* as I am thinking about this day and night and begin to lose the last hope. Alas! my dear Captain, it is so hard to live without any hope!

But in February 1921 Natasha received letter from a friend headed 'Very Secret', and the contents gave her renewed hope for a while. It said:

> It has been elucidated from the information received by the Ministry of Colonies, that a man has appeared in the French colonies in Asia, who claims to be the Grand Duke Michael Alexandrovitch and who is trying to obtain a visa for Europe.
> Alexei Sergeievitch Matveiev and Biriukov have approached the French authorities and Mr Matveiev handed over to them a photograph of the Grand Duke. It appears that the *Prefecture* is handling this business with all possible speed and there are sufficient reasons to believe that the identity of Grand Duke could be confirmed.
> Full assistance and necessary measures will be taken by the authorities, but in view of the distance of the place it will take some considerable time, such as 6 weeks or 2 months when the results will be known.*

But in September 1919 a copy of a telegram from Admiral Kolchak had been sent to her after she had made enquiries as to the whereabouts of Michael:

> In reply to the letter of Countess Brassow, please inform her that:
> > All information I possess does not give any indication that the Grand Duke Michael Alexandrovitch is at present in Siberia or the Far East. His fate is quite unknown after he was taken away in July last year and all attempts to find out where he was did not give any results. . . .
> >   Signed: Admiral Kolchak
> >   (Supreme Commander of the White Armies.)

So Natasha did not know what to believe. She tried to go on hoping, and she wrote to the captain:

> . . . of course I *have* to hope otherwise it is too hard to live! . . . I sometimes feel so depressed and tired of life and

---

* See Appendix.

think it is better to die, than to live such a miserable and aimless life. But I try not to complain and have always a smiling face. . . .

To add to all her worries money was now running short. Captain John Litchfield, the son of Captain Litchfield-Speer, remembers as a boy driving up Bond Street with Natasha in her Rolls-Royce. They stopped outside one of the big jewellers and he waited while Natasha went into the shop to sell an enormous pearl. Michael had owned some sugar factories in the Ukraine, and Natasha had received word that there were one hundred thousand roubles waiting to be transferred to England for her, but she had no idea of how to arrange the transfer of this money, and it was a terrible worry to her. The Litchfield-Speers were busy with their own lives and as time went by, seemed to have less and less time for visits to Snape. The truth was that Natasha was finding it different being in England alone without Michael. Before, in the years between 1912 and 1914, and especially during the time that they had been at Knebworth, they had been sought after by the very 'best' people. With the Grand Duke beside her as her legal husband, she had been accepted into Society along with him, even if sometimes her hostesses secretly disapproved of her. But now it was a different matter.

She had hoped, on arriving in England, that things would continue in more or less the same way, but after a while she began to understand the truth. She, Countess Brassow, was no one without her husband. It was true that a few friends still remained faithful to her and kept in close touch with her, but it was not the same at all. Gradually, in her mounting desperation, she sometimes succeeded in alienating even them by her demanding behaviour. She became jealous of their attentions to others; she resented their accepting invitations to functions to which she had not been invited. So to show the world that she did not care, she began to draw around her a type of person whom she would never have considered knowing in the old days. Rather than sit alone, she wined and dined them and they, being thrilled at knowing the wife of the Grand Duke Michael of Russia, flattered her from morning to night. Natasha became more and more haughty and arrogant, and succeeded in estranging even her dear friends the Litchfield-Speers. In April 1920 she wrote to the captain:

> I hope that Mrs Litchfield-Speer and you are not very angry with me that I asked you not to come today. You are coming here so seldom, that it is not worth indeed to come for a couple of hours. I want to see more and I am sorry to notice that it is not the same from your part. I see very well that when it concerns me you are always ill or very busy, for all your other engagements you seem to be alright. I am very sorry, but what can I do? I still hope one day you will be free enough to come to Snape. . . . With my kindest regards, your ex-friend, N. Brassow.

Apparently this letter had the desired effect, for she wrote afterwards:

> Thank you very much for your note which I was glad to receive. I am pleased to see that my letter had good results and you at once came to see me! In the future I shall always use this means of making you come and see me! No really, my dearest Captain, I am so sorry to see sometimes that you have changed towards me! But if you want to prove the contrary, you have to take me, as you have promised, for a drive in your beautiful new open car. It is the greatest pleasure for me to drive in an open car and now

since such a long time I am deprived of it. . . .

It is not really surprising that the Litchfield-Speers had cooled towards her, for earlier that month she had asked them if she could rent their house furnished for the summer months, and she had not been very polite about it:

> I remember your house very well, it is a nice one, only the bedrooms are too small, but for a short summer time I won't mind it. It is a house probably dreadfully cold in winter.

She saw less and less of the Litchfield-Speers:

> It is ages since I saw or heard of you and it was a real pleasure to get your letter . . . you are always so busy and there are so many complications to see you, so of course we gradually lose sight of each other. We really seem to live in different countries and I see more often people who are living in France than you, but there is nothing to do, such is life! . . .

15 Exile—France

At the end of 1920 Natasha and her children moved from Snape to Percy Lodge, East Sheen, and Tata started to attend Cheltenham Ladies' College. However, she soon managed to persuade her mother that it was time that she left school and suggested that she should take a secretarial course at Wimbledon, and after a lot of arguing Natasha eventually agreed to this. One day, at a lunch party, Tata was introduced to an Oxford undergraduate called Val Gielgud and they fell most romantically in love. Tata did not dare to tell Natasha that she had a boy friend as in those days well-brought-up Russian girls just did not have the freedom and tolerance that their English counterparts enjoyed, but nevertheless she and Val managed to meet quite frequently. They went for walks together in Richmond Park and sometimes they used to sit for hours in a cinema holding hands in the dark when Natasha went for the day to London. Natasha knew nothing of all this. Then one day Val proposed marriage to Tata and she accepted; they both thought that the time had come to introduce him to Natasha. Natasha received him coldly and on learning that he was penniless, showed him the door and forbade Tata ever to see him again.* But Tata

* . . . she took a very poor view of me! I can remember the exceptional

was her mother's daughter and such a ban only made her all the more determined to marry Val, and it is strange that Natasha, of all the people in the world, failed to recognize this side of herself in her daughter. But the relationship between the two of them was not very good at this time; the two high-spirited women were getting on each other's nerves, and Natasha must have been so irritated by her eighteen-year-old daughter that she did not stop to think. So Tata refused to give in, and as she needed a parent's permission to marry as she was still under age, she wrote to her father from whom she had heard recently, and asked him for his consent to her marriage. Mamontoff sent his permission and sent a small gift of money with his love and best wishes. On 12th August 1921 Val and Tata were married secretly at the Registry Office in Kensington. That same evening she returned home and said nothing to her mother about her marriage. She wore her wedding ring on a chain around her neck, well out of sight. She was determined to keep it a secret, as Val was in no financial position to support a wife and he wanted to keep the marriage a secret from his people as well. But a few weeks later yet another row broke out between mother and daughter, and Tata forgot herself in the heat of the argument and answered her mother back. Natasha said that she would send Tata away to a convent in Belgium to teach her some manners as clearly she had none at all; Tata replied that she could do no such thing as she (Tata) was now a married woman, and to prove it she showed her mother the ring on its chain round her neck, and then produced her marriage certificate. Natasha

beauty of a face still young under snow-white hair; and her rings, which were solitaire – an emerald, a diamond, and a sapphire; out of this world!'
Extract from a letter from Val Gielgud, 1972.

was absolutely furious and replied that as Tata was now a married woman, her place was with her husband and that she was to leave immediately. Amid much shouting and slamming of doors Tata packed her cases and left home.

After Tata had left, Natasha decided to move from Percy Lodge. She took a lease of a house at 26 Bolton Gardens, in Kensington, and started living an even more social life. She entertained lavishly and often gave the most marvellous parties. She hired the services of an excellent cook whom she paid 17/6 per week, and a little housemaid whom she paid 7/6 per week. In 1924 George left his preparatory school and went to Harrow where he shared a room in the Headmaster's House with two other boys – it was known as a threesome. George was immediately nicknamed 'Brass-OW' with the emphasis on the last syllable. One of his roommates remembers him as being a small boy for his age and with a rather pale complexion. He was often bullied and teased as he would not stand up for himself, but bullying was not really a bad problem in the Headmaster's House.

Gradually Natasha had to admit to herself that her financial state was deteriorating fast and that she could no longer go on living in the style that she had been enjoying – and recently actually 'enjoying' less and less. She very often felt desperately lonely, even in the middle of one of her parties. Most of her so-called friends, she had realized, had nothing really in common with her. They were just there for the champagne and caviar that she served so lavishly. A day did not pass in which she did not long for Misha and their happy times together, those days when money too flowed like the champagne was flowing now. George was a comfort, but now he had it in his head to leave Harrow, as he felt that it was stupid to waste so much money on providing him with an education that would be no use to him in the future, as it would do nothing to help him to earn his living in a competitive society later on. But Natasha wanted her son to be brought up as a Prince, even though she could not afford it, and she would not listen to reason.

One day she decided to move to Paris to live. Many of her Russian friends had chosen to settle in France rather than in England, and most important of all, life was cheaper in France in those days, and she would not be obliged to lose face in front of all her English friends whom she had been wining and dining so lavishly. She would be able to start living on a more modest scale in Paris right from the start; it would be a compromise. She wrote to her friend Captain Litchfield-Speer:

> . . . and there is a question now of my moving to Paris. The life is three times expensiver here than in France, and all revenue I should be able to get from our Polish Estate and sugar factories will be only in *francs*, so you see I will lose a lot!

So it was that in 1926 she moved to Paris. She put most of her belongings into a depository in London, and took only the necessary things to Paris with her. Some friends of hers, a Monsieur and Madame Tukine owned a large house at 9 rue Berlioz, just off the Avenue Malakoff in the sixteenth *arrondissement,* and they kindly let her have a whole floor to herself as an apartment, and she paid them a nominal rent.

The following year George left Harrow and continued his education in France at a school that was often known as the French Eton – Ecole des Roches at Verneuil, in the department of Eure. Verneuil is a small town about fifty miles west of Paris. The surrounding countryside is not very interesting, and in those days the chief local industries were farming and cider-making.

George arrived there, shy and lonely in September 1927, but pleased to have left Harrow which he hated. He soon made friends with two English brothers who were the only English pupils there at that time, and they immediately nicknamed him 'Brass'. This amused and pleased him, as Natasha had been insisting that everyone, including his close friends, address him as 'Prince' and this irked and upset him. All he wanted was to be able to live the life of a normal boy, and so to be called 'Brass', affectionately by his two friends, which was quite different from the disdainful 'Brass-OW' of Harrow, was something he found delightful.

The days passed quickly and George soon settled into the school routine. On rising in the mornings, the boys had to take a cold shower unless excused on health grounds, and this and sports were the things that George disliked most of all. The quality of the school food was not too bad, but the boys felt that where it failed was in quantity.

As there was no Orthodox Church in the vicinity, George would attend Roman Catholic religious instruction but Protestant services; as he put it, the former was most interesting and the latter's services were shorter and less frequent. He used to say that religious denominations could be classed as follows:- Protestant Porks, Orthodox Oxen, Catholic Cats, and Methodist Monkeys.

During their free time they used to go for cycle rides,

and sometimes they would buy cider from the local farms at 2 francs a litre (the rate of exchange was 240 f. for £1 in those days). Their pleasure in drinking quantities of this cider was by no means diminished by watching the making of it. The fact that men and women would walk bare-foot across a dung-covered farm yard, climb on to the press and solemnly tread down the well-rotted apples with their dirty feet did not put them off at all. Sometimes the three friends would buy some cherries as well, and cycle into some woods where they would sit on a log and see which of them could spit the cherry stones the farthest.

One day George bought himself a powerful motorcycle, a Norton, and would ride it at high speeds around the countryside. It was almost as if he were trying to escape from himself, to find a freedom of expression that he was not allowed to have by his Mamma. She was still insisting that everyone should pay him reverence due to his rank, and wanted him to live as a royal prince at all times. So George found a kind of freedom in the saddle of his Norton as he rushed round the lanes, and in spitting cherry stones with his two English friends.

Natasha was less lonely in Paris than she had been in London, especially as she had many old friends among the large Russian *émigré* community there. She was granted the title of 'Princess' by the Grand Duke Cyril, who was the recognized living head of the Romanoff family at that time. Tata was often in Paris too. Her marriage to Val Gielgud had not lasted very long, and in 1923 they parted. The circumstances of their courtship and marriage had been too romantic, and the romance had soon faded away, worn thin by money worries, shabby flats and tinned tongue for supper.

Tata began to model dresses as a free-lance mannequin, first in London and then later in Paris for Patou; she was one of the mannequins who helped to launch the revolutionary cocktail pyjamas which caused such a furore.

Eventually Tata's divorce from Val was finalized and she returned to England and married Cecil Gray, the music critic and writer, for the security from money worries that he offered her.

Natasha thoroughly approved of this marriage, and hoped and believed that her daughter had finally settled down. When in 1929 Tata gave birth to a daughter, Natasha at once came to London from Paris to see her first grandchild. She was thrilled at being a grandmother. But it was not long before the two women were arguing again together over the proper care to give a baby. My mother wanted to give me pure orange juice in a bottle. Natasha was horrified and tried to snatch the bottle away. Tata shouted at her mother, Natasha went upstairs and slammed the door of her room and did not come downstairs for half an hour. Natasha decided to return to Paris. It was obvious that mother and daughter still could not get on well together, though they had by now a great affection and respect for each other.

George was, I have been told, very proud of being an uncle, and often used to visit his sister at her home in London and would sit me on his lap and make funny noises at me. He left Les Roches and started studying for his *baccalauréat* at the Sorbonne in Paris. During the summer of 1930 George and Tata went to Cannes together for a holiday. Tata had many friends there, and though they were all much older than George, he seemed to fit in very well with everyone, and it was not long before he made many friends of his own age. He had brought his beloved Norton with him to Cannes, and he dearly loved to ride it at speed all over the place. One very hot day he was riding it along the sea front from Cannes to La Napoule when he must have fallen asleep for a second. The motor-bike fell over and George skidded on his back on the road for a short distance. He was lucky to escape without any serious injury – just a few bruises and a grazed back. Tata was very cross with him and lectured him on the danger of speed.

George was by now twenty years old, a handsome young man. He looked very much like his father, and had fair hair and blue eyes and was the same height and had the same slim figure and small waist. There were some people who, despite the fact that he was the child of a morganatic marriage, looked on George as the heir to the Throne of Russia – for after all, had not his father been the last Tsar? But George paid no attention to the claims made on his behalf; he was completely indifferent and half-amused by it all. Like his father, he was not a political animal, and like his father all he wanted was to be left alone to live his own life. He had simple tastes in food, he did not smoke and hardly ever drank anything stronger than cider, and though he occasionally took a girl out to tea or to the cinema, he never appeared to feel very strongly about her; he was always charming and solicitous towards girls, but not one of them every managed to inspire him deeply.

In 1931 George bought himself a Chrysler sports car and loved it dearly. On one occasion he offered to drive Tata from Paris to Boulogne, as she was returning to

England from a visit to Paris. But Tata refused the offer. She hated the speed at which George insisted on driving, and felt happier and safer travelling on the boat-train.

Natasha was worried as well about the way in which George had taken to driving his car, but whenever she tried to remonstrate with him, he just told her gently to stop fussing. Another of her worries was her financial situation; it was becoming worse as time went by. Most of her Russian friends were in the same position, and sometimes they would laugh together at their *petites économies*, and at how different it was from the old days when they had automatically ordered the most expensive cuts of meat, the very best materials without asking the cost. In the afternoons several of her friends would meet to play *bézique*, and they would take it in turns to be the hostess. They would talk and gossip as much as they played cards and drink glasses of tea and nibble biscuits. Every Easter they would attend the midnight service at the Russian church in the rue Daru, and weep gently as they listened to the beautiful music which so reminded them of their happy carefree days at home in Russia. After the service was over, they sometimes allowed themselves to be persuaded to drink a glass of vodka and to eat some *piroshki* in the little Russian café opposite the church.

Occasionally even now, there would arise some rumours to the effect that Michael had been heard of alive, and well, in China* or some such place, and for a while she would experience hope. It seems strange to us in the nineteen-seventies to realize that there could actually have been still any hope alive in the early nine-

* See Appendix

teen-thirties. It was not just Natasha who hoped and who went on hoping. It was endemic among the whole White Russian community. Their hopes were kindled by rumours of the wildest kind, and were fed on by their own unquenchable Russian optimism and spirit. But one afternoon Natasha overheard a conversation in a tea-room where she was sitting, resting after a walk. The tea-room was full of her compatriots, and on entering she had been greeted by many friends and acquaintances. Then, at the next table to her she heard the following conversation in Russian between two men. It concerned a third man, a Monsieur B:

1st man: Isn't it terrible about B-?
2nd man: Why; what has happened?
1st man: They say that he was taken by the Reds, disembowelled, and left to bleed to death, hanging on a tree.
2nd man: Shush! Do be quiet! He's sitting at the next table, and he will hear you!

After that, Natasha never again paid any attention to rumours.

She often attended the services at the Russian church. One Sunday, accompanied by her friend Princess Eristoff she was just entering the church when the Grand Duke Cyril pushed past her and walked down the aisle in front of her to his seat. Princess Eristoff was very cross. She told Natasha that, according to protocol, she (Natasha) should walk in front of the Grand Duke Cyril, for had not Natasha been the consort of the last Emperor of Russia, even if his reign had lasted for only twenty-four hours? But Natasha just shrugged her shoulders. It was rude in any case to push past a woman in that fashion whether she was an emperor's wife or a bank-clerk's wife . . . she did not intend making a scene in front of such ignorance. . . .

It cannot be said that Natasha was popular among the other members of the Russian community. She had a reputation for being impatient and arrogant, and many were afraid of her quick and sarcastic tongue. She was inclined to speak her mind, loudly and clearly, and did not care if she hurt people in the process. If reproached for this, she would defend herself by maintaining that she was only being truthful, which after all was a virtue, was it not? She was particularly scathing towards women who were unfortunate enough to incur her displeasure by being considered attractive, and she would enumerate their bad points loudly, for all to hear. She had developed, in her middle age, a high standard of moral behaviour and expected everyone to live up to it. Woe betide those who did not, for they would soon hear her scorn! But she was a loyal and good friend to many, and was much loved and admired by a circle of people.

One morning, in the middle of July 1931, George called on his mother with a young friend. They were on their way to Cannes, having finished sitting for their *baccalauréat* they felt in need of a holiday. They told Natasha that they were going to take it in turns to drive George's Sports Chrysler, and George promised his mother to be back for his twenty-first birthday which was in two weeks' time. Natasha gave the two boys something to eat, and then waved to them as they drove off around the corner with the engine revving loudly and the tyres squealing. Afterwards she maintained that she had felt a moment of premonition of danger as she winced at the noise that they made as they drove off in such high spirits. A few hours later, during that afternoon, the telephone rang in her apartment. She was in the middle of a game of *bézique* with a few friends, and she had been in a happy mood and had been laughing and joking with them. There was no premonition of disaster at all as she lifted the receiver and said 'Hallo?'. It was a call from a hospital at Sens, informing her that George was lying injured and unconscious there. The sports car had skidded into a tree and the other young man had been killed instantly. George was still alive, though not expected to survive for much longer. Her friends helped her to call a taxi and accompanied her to the Gare de Lyons, bought her a ticket and saw her on to the first train to Sens. She eventually arrived at the hospital just before midnight. George was still unconscious. She sat by his bed all night, stroking his forehead and talking to him all the while in Russian, French and English. When morning came George died from internal injuries without regaining consciousness.

Natasha returned to Paris with his body. With the little money she still possessed she bought two freehold plots (*à perpétuité*) in the fashionable cemetery at Passy in Paris; in one George was buried, the other one she intended to keep for herself, so that one day she would lie next to him.

The feelings of the Russian community in Paris were mixed. Almost everyone felt deeply for the poor bereaved mother, and they mourned sincerely with her for the loss of such a charming and handsome young man, the son of the brother of their Emperor. But there were people who gloated secretly over this new blow to the beautiful Princess Brassow. Natasha's enemies had been hoping for a long time to see this arrogant woman humbled, but they were disappointed. She refused to show her grief in public, and her amazing courage which she had never lacked helped her to survive those terrible weeks after George's death. Wherever she went during that period, she was seen to be composed, though somewhat pale-faced. She held her back straight as usual and her head up as she walked. Some people thought that she was completely heartless and cold. They did not know how she would rush to the apartment of the Princess Eristoff at odd times of the day, in order to be able to give way to her grief. For hours on end she would cry: 'What is there left for me now?' 'Why should I go on living? My son! My son! My son! I cannot bear it! Oh Misha! Oh Georgie! What can I do? How can I go on living?' and she would weep and weep. Princess Eristoff would weep too and try in vain to console her friend, but there was nothing she could do to say or help. Eventually Natasha would cease her terrible crying, drink a glass of tea, and then leave, eyes dry, back held straight, head held high, to return to her empty apartment.

Natasha was now completely penniless. All the last years she had been living mostly on capital, as the revenue from the Polish Estates was bringing in less and less. At first, in England, they had lived on a very lavish scale, because they were anticipating being able to return to Russia after a short while. In the same way as they had always hoped to see the Grand Duke alive and safe one day, they also thought that there would be a restoration of the monarchy. In Paris Natasha had lived much more frugally, but George's education and now the cost of his funeral, which had been on the grand scale necessary to accord with his position as the son of the Grand Duke Michael, had left her without any funds.

After George's death, Tata filed a claim on her mother's behalf against the Polish Government for annexing the Estates which had belonged to Michael. The Treaty of Riga in 1921 had allowed the Polish Government to take over any Russian Imperial property in their country. But it was Tata's contention that the treaty had been made after Michael's death; therefore as George was Michael's heir and as he was a commoner, the property was no longer 'Imperial' and therefore could not be annexed. Now that George was dead, Tata was his heir as they were children of a 'common womb' which was what counted in Napoleonic Law. Her case was that the Polish Government owed her for the property which was valued somewhere in the region of £600,000. The claim was for return or compensation. A group of international lawyers proposed to handle the case for a percentage, and were even prepared to go so far as to actually finance the case, and to subsidize Natasha until it was heard, so sure were they of winning. The case was eventually heard; Natasha lost.

In 1938 in London, an advertisement appeared in a daily newspaper one morning to the effect that if the goods belonging to the Princess Brassow were not claimed and the outstanding account paid, the firm who owned the depository concerned would be obliged to sell all the items to defray expenses hitherto incurred. Tata went to the depository and was presented with a bill of astronomical proportions which she was quite unable to settle, and she knew that it was out of the question for Natasha to pay this amount either. So Tata started to open the crates and trunks to see if there was anything of value which she could sell to help to pay the account. In an old glove-box, loosely tied with string, she was astonished to find a large number of what looked like regalia of various Orders of Chivalry, which must have belonged to the Grand Duke Michael. She took them home with her and immediately consulted a friend of hers, Charles Beard, who was an expert on heraldry. He identified and indexed them as follows:

> The Most Noble Order of the Garter. Collar, Badge, Star, Greater and Lesser Georges and Garter itself.
>
> The Order of the Bath, complete with Collar, in silver gilt.
>
> The Golden Fleece, sixteen ounces of gold.
>
> The Annunziata of Italy, light in weight, but of beautiful workmanship, in gold.
>
> The St. Andrew of Russia, an elaborate work in gold and enamel, with a heavy chain.
>
> The Badge of the Danish Order of the Elephant.
>
> The Collar and Star of the Norwegian St Olaf.
>
> The Siamese Order of the Maha Chakrakri.
>
> The Badge and Star of the Japanese Chrysanthemum.
>
> The Badge of the Portuguese Order of Christ and St Benedict.
>
> The Badge and Silver Collar of the House of Hohenzollern.
>
> The Badge and Collar of the Order of Merit of Oldenburg.

The regalia must have been forgotten at Knebworth in 1914 when war was declared and the family had packed up in a hurry to return to Russia; the old glove-box must have been put into store along with their other things. Through the years they must have been moved from Snape to Percy Lodge to Bolton Gardens and then back into store once more when Natasha went to Paris to live in 1926. For about twenty-four years they had remained lost. Their value was estimated at between £2,000 and £10,000 and it seemed as if at last Natasha's financial worries were over as she reluctantly gave her permission for these items to be sold—reluctantly, as she felt that, somehow, they were a link with Michael. They had been given to him to honour him. How could she sell his honour in order to buy groceries? But Tata and friends argued with her and pointed out that had Michael been alive, he would have been the first to suggest selling them. He would not have wanted her to starve while the means to alleviate hunger were there beside her. So, eventually she agreed.

A firm of auctioneers advanced £200 to clear the goods from the depository, and they published a special illustrated catalogue, announcing the 16th December as the date of the sale.

Then came a request from Denmark that their Order of the Elephant be withdrawn from the sale; they did not want it sold. Tata immediately returned it to them, as the family were for ever in great debt to the Danish Royal family for having looked after George as their own son during those early days of the revolution.
Then the Crown, through the Chancellor of the Orders of Knighthood claimed the Orders of the Garter and the Bath. Once it became known that the British Crown had claimed their Orders, claims began to pour in from other countries as well. The sale was cancelled only on the very morning that it was due to take place, and

when the sale-room was packed with people.

Some of the claims presented very difficult legal problems. The Nazi Government claimed the Hohenzollern, the Oldenburg and the Golden Fleece; but the question was, could a Republic claim a Royal Order? Then there were conflicting claims for the Golden Fleece; did it belong to Ex-Emperor Otto, (as it was an Austrian Order) Ex-King Alphonso (as it had been made in Spain), or to Adolf Hitler? I do not know what eventually happened to the Golden Fleece, but piece by piece the other Orders were returned to their owners. Only an oriental government made a payment of a small sum of money to Natasha for the return of their Order out of a sense of chivalry.

So after high hopes, Tata and Natasha were now in debt to the auctioneers. They found treasure for princes and were rewarded with a bill for incidental expenses. Among other boxes in the store were found some other saleable items. A golden flute fetched £100 when sold, and various *objets d'art* realized a small sum, which meant that all the debts were finally settled, but there was nothing left over at all for Natasha.

16 The End

Natasha lived her last years in a shabby little bed-sitting room in a top floor flat in the *Sèvres-Babylone* district of Paris. The flat was owned by an elderly Russian spinster named Mlle Annenkov, who was extremely rude and unpleasant to Natasha. I suppose that she was jealous and had, in the past, envied Natasha's life and loves, glamour and position. But things had changed, and it was now her turn to wield the power over this once proud woman, and so she took pleasure in treating Natasha like dirt, and in being as rude as she possibly could. She knew very well that Natasha had no alternative but to accept quietly and resignedly everything that she might say to do, for she had nowhere else to go. It makes my mind reel when I try to appreciate what it must have cost Natasha to accept this situation. What superb self-control she must have discovered in herself! Natasha Brassow had finally learned to curb her tongue and control her temper!

My Mamontoff cousins rember Natasha visiting them from time to time during this period; no doubt she wanted to escape from the Annenkov for a while. Sometimes she would appear wearing trousers, which was considered very eccentric in those days for an elderly lady, and very dashing and elegant she looked too. Her visits were at first a great surprise to the Mamontoffs; in the past, when she had been the consort of a Grand Duke, Natasha had been far too high and mighty to have anything to do with the family of her first husband. But the Mamontoffs are very kind and understanding people, and so they welcomed her cordially and gave her tea and drink and things to eat as she looked so pale and thin, and then they would sit and talk about old times until Natasha had to return to the old Annenkov.

Meanwhile Tata's marriage to Cecil Gray had proved to be no more successful than hers to Val had. In the winter of 1932 Tata had been seriously ill with a form of meningitis. She recovered eventually and so made medical history as she was one of three known cases of recovery from this particular type of meningitis. So, in February 1933 it was decided to send her to her beloved Cannes for a holiday to convalesce. Cecil stayed at home in London to keep an eye on my nursemaid and on me. It was while she was in Cannes that she met again Michael Majolier who, strange as it may seem, had been a midshipman on board *HMS Agamemnon* in 1918 on the journey from Constantinople to Malta. It seemed so natural that they should spend a great deal of the time together, and by the end of the holiday, when Tata had to return to London they realized that they were passionately in love with each other. So Tata returned home and confessed all to her husband. After a great deal of shouting and slamming of doors (history *does* repeat itself!) she left her husband and little daughter and went off to live with and eventually marry Michael Majolier. In leaving Cecil she left behind her a way of life that spelled security from money worries, and in its place inherited a life of deep love and devotion, but one in which money troubles were normal and quotidian. I hope that the regrets that she voiced to me towards the end of her life were only superficial moans, but she died an embittered and unhappy old lady. However, that is another story . . . .

Natasha did not approve of this third marriage of her daughter's and did all she could to dissuade Tata from taking the step of leaving Gray to hitch her wagon to Majolier. But Tata was in love and refused absolutely to listen to any advice, and so she left not only a kind husband but also me.

I will however just mention something that I find most touching and which brings me near to tears whenever I remember. I was sent off to a boarding school at a young age, which was the obvious solution for my father, being left alone with a small daughter to look after; and each of my birthdays brought a birthday card signed in large, rather flamboyant writing 'from your Mamma'. Every birthday a card arrived without fail until the war. I am not quite sure as to exactly when these cards stopped arriving, but I think that the last one I received was in 1940. I thought that they were from my mother, and I was very pleased and thrilled that this almost unknown 'Mamma' remembered me and loved me enough to send me birthday cards. I was about three years old when I had last seen her, and I had only the vaguest memories of her. It was only when I was fifteen years old and had met my mother again that I realized that her handwriting in no way resembled the flamboyant foreign writing on those birthday cards. Indeed, it was much later on when I met my grandmother again and started to correspond with her that I understood the truth. It was Natasha who had sent me the cards each year; not my mother. Natasha had guessed that Tata would not have bothered to do such a thing, but she had not wanted me to know this. She could easily have signed the cards 'from your Grandmamma' and I would still have been pleased. But she did not want me to feel that I was completely forgotten by my mother. I find this very touching.

The Nazi occupation of Paris brought with it some hopes to Natasha, for were not the Germans the enemies of Soviet Russia? The Grand Duchess Olga wrote in her memoirs: '. . . they (the White Russians) did not profess the Nazi creed, but they were compelled by their conscience to join the Germans because, as they believed, it was a chance to free Russia from Communism. As I know only too well, many thousands of those *emigrés*, settled in Allied countries, were faced with a terrible dilemma, but what possible choice could they have when the Allies were on Stalin's side? . . . Hitler kept saying that he meant to free my country from the Reds. . . .'

After the war, in 1946 I went to Paris and met my grandmother again for the first time since I was a child. I was upset at her plight. She did not complain at all but I could see that she was starving, and her clothes, though clean and well-pressed, were very shabby. Her poor little gloves were more darns than material. I had great difficulty in making her tell me exactly what her financial situation was. One afternoon, when we were sitting together in her bed-sitting room, and the old

Annenkov was trying to listen at the door to hear what we were saying about her, I tried to make Natasha talk about money, but she would only talk about the old wood-burning stove in her room which was her only method of heating. She would put some pieces of wood into it and then swear in Russian as smoke would appear from every possible crack. Sometimes the stove would actually go out altogether, and at this Natasha would become absolutely furious. It was as if the stove had taken on a personality to her and had become an evil monster working against her all the time. But after a lot of gentle bullying on my part she admitted that she was existing, and only just, in deepest poverty. She had sold everything of value. Occasionally at irregular intervals an exiled compatriot* would, for old time's sake, let her have small sums of money. This was literally all she had to live on.

When I returned to London I took the necessary steps to obtain special permission from the Bank of England, which was needed in those days, to send her as my dependant relative, the sum of £4 per month which was all I could afford from my salary of £20 per month which was what I earned as a typist in London. My mother was herself having a difficult time making ends meet with Majolier, and could do nothing to help. It is quite true that £4 then bought much more than it does today, but no one would pretend that it was riches; but at least it was a regular income and Natasha did not have to actually starve any more.

At the end of 1951 she began to suffer from illness and pain. The trouble was diagnosed as cancer of the breast, and when Mlle Annenkov heard of it she threw Natasha

* Youssoupoff, I think.

out of her flat. She was not prepared to look after an invalid and have all the bother and unpleasantness. Princess Eristoff begged Mlle Annenkov to reconsider, but she had made up her mind. So Natasha, sick and in pain and now homeless, was taken to a charity ward of a nearby hospital where she died on 23rd January 1952. The whole Russian community turned out for her funeral, and generously heaped magnificent flowers on her coffin. I could not help wondering what good all those lovely flowers were to Natasha now that she was dead. Would it not have been a finer gesture to have done something for her while she was alive and starving? However . . . that is life, and that is death. So Natasha was buried in the smart cemetery at Passy, next to her Georgie as she had wanted, but with only a plain wooden cross to mark her grave as there simply was no money to pay for a headstone.

In 1956 I visited the cemetery and found her grave covered with long grass and looking very shabby among all the other large and ornate tombs. Soon after this my mother had the idea of trying to arrange to have Natasha's and George's bodies exhumed, taken to the Russian Cemetery at St Geneviève des Bois, near Paris, and re-interred there; she proposed to sell the two freehold plots at Passy for a large sum and to use the money to erect suitable tombstones of marble in the Russian cemetery. As I was often in Paris at that time, she asked me to arrange all this. I refused. Firstly I felt that as Natasha had bought those two plots at Passy for George and for herself, that was where she had chosen to be, and secondly I did not want to dig up my grandmother. Let her rest in peace, I thought. I mentioned all this to my Aunt Maroussia Mamontoff, thinking that she would agree with me, but to my surprise she did not, though for a different reason. 'But what is there for them at Passy all on their own?' she said, 'Poor things! How lonely they must be! It would be far better for them to be at St Geneviève where at least they would be among friends!' *Mais qu'est ce qu'ils peuvent faire tous seuls à Passy'* is what she actually said in French. It does not really mean 'what can they do?' but it comes very near to it. It conjures up a vision of great activities in the cemetery after dark; of parties and receptions among the inmates; and that at Passy, George and Natasha would have been left out of it all, forgotten and uninvited by their merry-making friends at St Geneviève. . . . Though I am half Russian I am also half Scots, and it must have been the Scottish side in me that would not let me change my mind, and so George and his mother stayed on undisturbed, and I hope in peace, at Passy.

In the 1960s I was too busy having babies in England to find the time to go to Paris. In 1971 however I went back to Paris and visited the cemetery at Passy to see what sort of state her poor little grave was in. I was astounded to find a magnificent marble tomb with her name and George's and *'Fils et Epouse de S.A.I. Grand Duc Michel de Russie'* engraved in gold letters upon it. I immediately went to see the cemetery keeper in his little office at the gate, to ask him how this extraordinary thing had come about. The keeper and his assistant wore black tail-coats and old-fashioned wing collars, and as the office had a highly polished parquet floor and as they wished to protect it from unnecessary wear and tear, they were in the habit of using pieces of felt under their shoes to move about on. When I asked the keeper about the new monument that I had found at my grandmother's grave, he skated across the office on two bits of felt, coat-tails swinging jauntily behind him, over to some shelves and took down a bulky dusty file. After having taken out some letters and documents and read them, he told me the following story.

It seems that in 1965 a Soviet Russian had visited the cemetery. He had not stayed long, and on leaving he had entered the office and had said to the keeper that he did not think much of the White Russian community if they were content to leave the grave of the wife and son of the Grand Duke Michael in such terrible condition. He then left. A few days later the keeper repeated this to the by now rather elderly Princess Eristoff. She was so incensed and offended by this criticism coming as it did from a 'sale Bolshevik' that she immediately set about organizing a collection among the Russian community, especially among the surviving army officers. After a few years, they managed to save enough money to pay for the marble monument.

Who was this Soviet Russian who was so concerned over the state of Natasha and George's grave? Who could it have been? It is very strange for one would not think that it could possibly be of interest to anyone in the U.S.S.R. Perhaps his surname could throw some light on the mystery, but unfortunately I could not find out what it was. Who knows, perhaps it was Mamontoff, (there are still some in Russia), or Cheremetevsky .... Could it have been Milyukov, Gutchkov, Shulgin, Rodzyanko, or even possibly Kerensky? I wish I knew. . . .

As I was leaving the cemetery that day in 1971 I noticed quite near to Natasha's grave, the tomb of Maurice Paléologue, the former French Ambassador to Russia, who had so admired Natasha in a St Petersburg shop in those far off days in 1915. . . .

17 Ifs and Buts, and Might-Have-Beens

When Nicholas abdicated for himself and for his son in favour of his brother Michael, he in fact committed an unlawful act. The laws of Russia at that time did not envisage the possibility of the abdication of a ruling emperor and gave no guidelines concerning the succession to the throne in such a case. Since the result of abdication is the same as death, then the throne should have passed to the lawful heir. Nicholas had absolutely no right to deprive his son of the throne; it was not his private property for him to dispose of and give away as he wished. Thus Michael had no legal right to the throne whatsoever, and the only right recourse would have been to adhere to the ordinary laws of succession which would have followed Nicholas's death; Alexis would have become Tsar, and Michael would have been to adhere to the ordinary laws of succession which would have followed Nicholas's death; 'that it (this reasoning) had an effect on Michael's thinking.'

Nabokov goes on to say: '. . . I ask myself whether there might have been a better chance of a favourable outcome (to create a new Russia) if Michael Alexandrovitch had accepted the crown from the Tsar's hands. . . .' His argument was that acceptance would have preserved the machinery and structure of government. The basis of Russia's state system would have been saved, and all the essentials would have been there to guarantee a constitutional monarchy. The great shock to the nation, caused by the collapse of the throne, would have been avoided. 'In short, the revolution would have been kept within bounds and the international position of Russia might have been saved. There was a chance of salvaging the army. . . .'

But Nabokov admits that this is only one side of the question. For Michael's acceptance to have been decisive, there would have to have been a number of conditions which were just not there. By accepting the throne from Nicholas, he would at once have aligned against himself those forces which stood at the fore in the first days of the revolution, and which sought to take control by means of close contact with the troops of the Petrograd garrison. By that time (3rd March) the minds of these mutinying troops had already been poisoned. They offered no real support. 'The consolidation of Michael's position would undoubtedly have called for resolute measures – not excluding bloodshed, the arrest of the Executive Committee of the Soviet Workers' and Soldiers' Deputies, and the proclamation of a state of siege in the event of resistance. Everything would probably have been reduced to proper proportions in a week. But for that week it would have been necessary to have at one's disposal actual forces in which complete and total reliance could be placed. No such forces existed.'

And then there was Michael's character to consider. All the contemporary historians agree on this point; Michael was by nature totally unfitted for the difficult, responsible and dangerous role that had been thrust upon him. He was a quiet, sensitive man, not over-endowed with intellect, who only asked to be left alone with his family far away from the ceremonial pomp at Court which he despised. He loved Russia deeply, and he had written in his diary on 2nd September 1917: 'Woke this morning to hear the proclamation of Russia as a Democratic Republic. Is it not all the same, whatever the shape of the government, so long as there be order, and justice, for everybody?' Outside his family he also loved his Division. He had made a long study of the manners and customs of the wild Caucasians whom he commanded, and as a result the men revered him. As a landlord of a country estate, he was conscientious to a fault and took special care of those of his tenants who were ill or in any kind of trouble. He knew all of them by name and was godfather to hundreds of them, remembering their birthdays and name-days with small gifts. But it was not enough to enable him to take the helm at this time in Russia's history; what was needed then was a strong hand, a ruthless personality, and Michael was unable to offer help to his country. Nabokov wrote: 'If Michael's acceptance of the throne had been possible, it would have been beneficial or at least it would have given hope for a happy outcome. But unfortunately the sum total of conditions was such that an acceptance of the throne was impossible. In common parlance, 'it wouldn't have come to anything.' And from the start Michael himself must have felt this. If 'we all have an eye to become Napoleons' he had the least inclination of all. It is curious to note that he particularly emphasized his resentment at his brother's 'foisting' the throne on him without even asking his consent. And Nabokov then asked:'... one wonders what he would have done if Nicholas *had* asked his consent beforehand?' An interesting speculation.

But what about Natasha in all this? I have already quoted Nabokov as having written: '... I ask myself whether there might have been a better chance of a favourable outcome if Michael Alexandrovitch had accepted the crown from the Tsar's hands....' This proves to me that he had never met my grandmother. He must have known of her existence; he must have heard stories about her, for she was notorious. But it would appear that he discounted her entirely. Perhaps, if he thought about her at all, he imagined her in the rôle of little help-meet, staying well in the background. Did he see her as a quiet and steady influence on Michael? As a modest nonentity? As a beloved Empress?

Whatever decision Michael took on that fateful March 3rd, it was bound to be the wrong one for him. It could not have been otherwise. Even had he been one of those people who 'had an eye to become Napoleons' there would still have been no hope for him or for Russia. Had he had the strength of a Caesar, or the verbal prodigality of a Churchill as well, it would not have made the slightest difference – Natasha was his consort, and that fact alone would have been enough to damn him. The moment he met the bold and beautiful Nathalia Cheremetevskaya he was doomed, and so was Imperial Russia.

Acknowledgements

It sometimes seems to me that there are times in one's life when one has no choice at all as to the action one will decide to take. This book then is the result of such a time; it exists because I had no choice whatsoever. It was inevitable, given the circumstances.

It all started when my mother died in 1969, and we found a large leather trunk in the basement of her house. It was full of the most fascinating photographs of her mother's life. For about twelve months I looked at them, showed them to friends, and thought about them. I believe that I was beginning to realize that I should do something about them. But what? Then early in 1971 another correspondence started up in the *Times* about Mr. Guy Richard's theory that the Russian Imperial family are still alive. The *Times* published the following letter:

> Sir, Mr. Guy Richards (March 27) is quite wrong in stating that 'four Romanovs including the Czar shorn of his beard' were taken to Malta in H.M.S. *Agamemnon* in December 1918.
>
> My father was commanding H.M.S. *Agamemnon* at that time and I have a documentary and photographic record of his passengers. They were the Countess Brassow, the morganatic wife of the Grand Duke Michael (the Czar's

ACKNOWLEDGEMENTS

brother); Mlle Mamontov, her daughter by a previous marriage; and Princess Wiazemsky, her lady-in-waiting.

Yours faithfully
John Litchfield.

I was naturally very excited at seeing the mention of both my grandmother and my mother in the *Times*, and I telephoned to Captain Litchfield. He was very pleased to hear from Tata's elder daughter; he and Tata had been quite good friends in the days when their parents were corresponding, but since Tata's marriage to Val Gielgud they had lost touch completely. I do not think that Captain Litchfield even knew that Tata had had any children, and he certainly did not know that she was now dead. He kindly invited my husband and me to tea, and he showed us about ten letters that Natasha had written to his father in the years from 1919 to 1922. He also gave me two alabaster flower urns that she had left with his family for safe-keeping in 1921. So now I had not only photographs, but letters as well. I began to feel that I should try to write a book.

For quite a while I tried to ignore this idea, and told myself that it was quite beyond my capabilities, but the idea persisted, nevertheless. It became a conviction eventually after I returned from a visit to Paris in 1971. I had gone one day to the cemetery at Passy to take a photograph of the poor little unkempt grave that I had remembered; I felt that it would be ideal for my book, if I ever managed to write one.; it would make a remarkable contrast to the other photos that I had of her in her luxurious furs and jewels and Rolls-Royces. My astonishment on finding the ornate marble tomb can be imagined, and the story of the Soviet Russian who had paid a visit to the cemetery so intrigued me that I returned home determined to try to write a book about it all. My husband and friends continued to encourage me, so I began to read as many books on the period as I could find, and started to write some rough drafts.

Then my Aunt Alison Gray in Edinburgh asked me one day if I knew what had happened to the 'Russian papers' that my Scottish grandmother had purchased from my Russian one in the 1930s. Up to that moment, no one had told me about these papers, and I did not pay very much attention to their possible existence. In 1972, after having read a rough draft of mine, Prince Nikita Romanoff suggested that it might be a good idea to find more about George and his education and youth. I felt that this was excellent advice, and I arranged for an advertisement to be inserted in The *Times* which read as follows:

> Count George Brassow. Information sought about his school days at Harrow in 1920s. Also details about his mother.

Quite a number of people answered and I received a great deal of the sort of information that I had been hoping for. There was also a letter from a man called Granville who wrote that his family had some papers concerning George Brassow. When I contacted him and went to see him, he produced an old cardboard box full of letters, papers and official-looking documents, all in Russian. These were the 'Russian papers' that my Aunt Alison had referred to. It transpired that the Granvilles had bought the house that my Scottish grandmother lived in during the 1930s and in the garage there they had found an old safe which contained these papers. Apparently Gran had become ill

ACKNOWLEDGEMENTS

suddenly and had left the house in a hurry, never to return to it again. Her personal belongings had been sent on after her but the safe in the garage must have been overlooked.

The discovery of these papers, consisting of love letters from Michael to Natasha, rough drafts of telegrams, notes, lists and other items, is strange enough one would think. But it is not as strange as the discovery of Michael's personal diaries. I find that I am hesitating to describe how it was that they came to light. My sister decided to have a broken bed mended, and removed an old brown paper parcel which had been propping it up for many years, since the death of our mother, in fact, in 1969. When she opened the parcel, she found it contained the diaries. Why our mother used them to prop up this bed, we shall never know. . . .

I would like to thank various kind people for their help, in talking about their memories of my grandmother or of George, or in providing facts and in generally offering material and valuable criticism and encouragement. In Paris I am indebted to Princess Eristoff, Colonel Mestcherinoff, Monsieur Chatsky, and of course to all my Mamontoff relations. In England I thank the Earl of Arran, Dr. Tania Guercken, Val Gielgud, Douglas Pelly, Hugh Morgan Edgington, John Bescoby-Chambers, Richard Deacon, Marvin Lyons, and especially Felix Brenner. I also thank Prince Nikita Romanoff for his helpful suggestions, and Baroness Moura Budberg for her help in identifying some of the people and places in the photographs and for her nice remarks which encouraged me greatly. Thanks are also due to Lev Magerovsky and Nora Beeson for searching through the Archives of the

ACKNOWLEDGEMENTS

Russian and Eastern History Department at Columbia University for me. I owe a great deal to Michael Bakhroushin who painstakingly translated all the Russian private papers for me.

I want to thank especially warmly Captain John Litchfield for lending me the letters from Natasha to his father and for allowing me to quote from them. I also thank him and his family for having looked after the two alabaster flower urns for fifty years, just because Natasha gave them for safe-keeping. The urns must have been favourite possessions and they appear in many photographs of her as a young woman – perhaps they were presents from Michael. They are now in my house and have become favourite possessions of mine. They remind me of Natasha and are a part of the life and times of my Russian grandmother.

Appendix — Rumours

It is an amazing fact that even now, in the seventies, there are still rumours about what did really happen at Ekaterinburg in July 1918. As recently as 1973, Jeremy Thorpe was reported in the press to be seeking parliamentary means of raising the question in the House of Commons about the fate of Nicholas II and his family. It seems that his question was ruled out of order on the technicality that it dealt with past history. It had come to Mr Thorpe's notice that it was being alleged that the U.S. State Department or the British Foreign Office were withholding a document that could possibly give some definite information on the subject, that it indicated that the Tsar escaped alive from Ekaterinburg. But Mr. Thorpe's question was not allowed.

I, myself, have always believed the accounts that the Imperial family were murdered in the basement of the Ipatiev House, and that their bodies were disposed of in the way that has been described so many times. But I feel that it is only right to tell now the views that are held by many responsible people of various nationalities which differ widely from the accepted facts. I do not mean people who could have a financial interest in believing otherwise, for it is almost certain, in spite of official denials, that there are in fact funds which belonged to Imperial Russia in various banks – if not in the United Kingdom – then in France and Switzerland. Thus there could be some people who have their eyes firmly fixed on this wealth and its acquisition. It is not those people to whom I am referring, but rather to those who cannot possibly have any financial interests. There is the large band of researchers who, coldly and logically examine the reports and sift the evidence. They refuse to be influenced by history books; they will not blindly accept statements made by contemporary sources which might be prejudiced in one way or another.

Nobody will argue that there were plans to rescue the Imperial Family from their imprisonment at the Ipatiev House in Ekaterinburg. It is very understandable and right that there should have been plans made. Is it not one of the more endearing traits of the human race to aspire to heroism, to fight against the loaded dice, to dare to defy authority? Where historians' accounts differ is in deciding whether these efforts were successful or were failures. The first reaction to the news of the massacre was general disbelief. Again, one feels that this is the right reaction; would we not feel the same at such news concerning the British Royal Family? Surely we would cling to the hope that someone had got his facts all mixed up and wrong. So hope was present, and because there was hope, there were rumours. Some of them started even as early as January 1918, even before the Imperial Family had been taken to Ekaterinburg:

APPENDIX

FORMER CZAR AND FAMILY REPORTED TO HAVE ESCAPED. (San Francisco Chronicle)
London Jan 18. Nicholas Romanoff, the former Emperor and his family have escaped from their prison near Tobolsk, it is reported in Petrograd according to a Reuter despatch from the Russian capital. The report, the despatch adds, lacks confirmation.

Nicholas Romanoff and his family were removed to Tobolsk by the Kerensky Government last August. In October, the Romanoffs were taken to the Abolsk Monastery, some distance outside Tobolsk.

The Executive Committee of the Congress of Peasant's Deputies on Jan 13 adopted the resolution urging that the former Emperor be brought to Kronstadt or Petrograd. A despatch from Amsterdam on Tuesday reported that the German papers had said that the former Empress had become insane and was confined in a Sanatorium at Tobolsk. Her condition was reported to be hopeless.

Everyone agrees that the last time that the Imperial Family were seen alive was during the night of 17th–18th July 1918. From that time on, the accounts differ. In history books one can read the detailed account of an assassination, taken from books and reports by Wilton, Bykov and Sokolov. Wilton was the correspondent of the *Times*, and went to Ekaterinburg in May 1919 to report on the findings by Sokolov, the trained legal investigator, who had been selected by Admiral Kolchak to make a thorough investigation into the alleged assassination of the Imperial Family. I have already quoted from Bykov's book *The Last Days of Tsardom* when describing the end of the Grand Duke Michael. But Bykov's book was not an official Soviet version of what happened at Ekaterinburg. At the time of the alleged massacre, Bykov was only a minor member of the Ural Soviet – it was at a later date that he succeeded Bjeloborodov as chairman of the Ural Soviet. His book started life as an article in a book published in 1921 and called *The Workers' Revolution in the Urals*. Bykov's article was described as 'A summary of conversations with comrades who were in one way or another connected with events that concerned the family of the former Tsar, or took an active part in its execution and the destruction of its corpses.' A summary of the original article is in Bulygin's book *The Murder of the Romanoffs*. Later Bykov published a larger version of the article in book form, and drew freely on already published sources – Sokolov's memoirs, Gilliard's memoirs, etc. Many people therefore consider *The Last Days of Tsardom* as a volume of hearsay evidence from different sources, and as such cannot be judged completely reliable.

'I am certain that the assassination of the Czar and his family did not happen as Sokolov suggested,' wrote Richard Deacon to me recently, 'and that the Sokolov report was largely faked. . . .'

'Whatever happened to them (the Imperial Family),' wrote John Bescoby-Chambers in a letter to me, 'they were NOT killed in the cellar in the Ipatiev House. After two years intensive study of this aspect of the case I reach exactly the same conclusion as most modern researchers who look objectively at the evidence – that there is no proof of an assassination, nor proof of an escape either!! There are indications as to the possibility of an escape but that is all. . . . One must, I feel, accept that the Ekaterinburg murders did not take place in the manner and place that is accepted by many historians. The family may well have been slaughtered elsewhere – there is evidence that the Tsarina and the

APPENDIX

children were taken to Perm . . . at best one can only say that the family *disappeared* at Ekaterinburg, and that its members have not been seen since. . . . I used to believe implicitly in the Sokolov report until I started to study it; I then found that it contained more holes than a piece of Gruyère cheese . . . there is enough evidence on file to discredit largely Sokolov's findings . . . the mysterious and convenient disappearance of the 'relics' for instance, the forensic evidence on them, the ballistics aspects of the Ekaterinburg case . . . all point to an elaborately staged hoax. The Bolsheviks may well have laid many false trails – indeed it is known that they did – Sokolov followed the longest false trail of all and was then unable to complete his investigations. . . . There are rumours of a rescue attempt – but nothing concrete. Various people claim to have seen people who have seen people who have seen documents, and so on. And even if such a rescue attempt was made, there is no guarantee that it was successful. . . .'

This 'rescue' rumour began to circulate after the news of a massacre became generally known. It said that Nicholas, Alexandra, the Tsarevitch, and the four girls were smuggled out of the Ipatiev House to safety, some say initially by means of a secret tunnel, and that after a long and arduous journey in the back of lorries and on foot, they eventually reached Chungking on the Upper Yangtze. From there it is said that they made their way to Poland where they lived incognito for many years. It is alleged that Alexandra died in 1924, but that Nicholas lived until 1952; that Olga, Tatiana and Anastasia are now alive and well in the United States, and that Marie stayed on in Poland and that she is still living there in Warsaw. They say that the Tsarevitch is in New York, married and a father, and that before he legally reverted to the name of Alexei Nicholaievitch Romanoff, he was known as Colonel Michael Goleniewski.

This Colonel Goleniewski must be a most interesting person in his own right, apart from his royal pretensions. He was a secret agent and defected from the Polish Military Intelligence and was instrumental in exposing dozens of KGB operatives in the West, among them 'Kim' Philby. Recently a friend of Colonel Goleniewski in New York sent me the photograph of him that appears in this book. The sender wrote that this photo was taken on 21st August 1972 and is a picture of the Tsarevich, Alexei Nicholaievitch Romanoff. . . .

The people who believe that the Imperial family did escape from Ekaterinburg say that the proof lies in the behaviour of the Dowager Empress Marie during her journey from Russia to England in 1919. Her gaiety and high spirits at that time are put down to the fact that she had secret information that her son and his wife and family were safe at a certain place in hiding. In fact, while at Malta, the Dowager Empress confided to a young British Army Lieutenant called Robert Ingham that she knew where Nicholas was. (This was on April 27th 1919.) Ingham wrote later: '. . . Her Majesty began to talk about her son – the Czar – and told me that she was careful not to let others know, but that she knew where he was. H.I.M. was fully convinced that he had escaped and was in hiding at a certain place'. It is certainly, at the very least, proof that the 'rescue' rumour was believed, but it cannot be said to be any more than that.

There is no doubt that there were many groups of

APPENDIX

people who were conspiring together, trying to rescue the Tsar and his family from the Ipatiev House. Bykov wrote: 'From the first days of the Romanov's transfer to Ekaterinburg, there began to flock in monarchists in great numbers, beginning with half-crazy ladies, countesses and baronesses of every calibre and ending with nuns, clergy and representatives of foreign powers.' Notes were found inside loaves of bread and in bottles of milk which were messages of hope for the Imperial family: 'The hour of liberation is approaching . . .' and 'The time has come for action . . . your friends sleep no longer. . . .' On 27th June, Nicholas wrote in his diary: 'We spent an anxious night, and kept up our spirits, fully dressed. All this was because a few days ago we received two letters, one after the other, in which we were told to get ready to be rescued by some devoted people, but days passed and nothing happened and the waiting and the uncertainty were very painful.'

After 18th July 1918, the date that is given for the massacre at Ekaterinburg, the 'rescue' rumours started to be known internationally. On 7th December 1918 a cable was sent from the US Ambassador to Italy in Rome, Nelson Page, to the Secretary of State in Washington:

> For your confidential information, I learned in highest quarters here it is believed that the Czar and his family are all alive. Paris informed. Signed Nelson Page.

A few days later, on 16th December 1918, the *New York Times* quoted an Associated Press report:

> The mother of former Emperor Nicholas, who is living near Livadia in the Crimea, has been receiving letters every ten days purported to come from the former ruler,

according to Polish officers who have arrived here (Warsaw) from Sebastopol.

On Christmas Eve that year the *New York Times* quoted another Associated Press report:

> "There is no doubt that the Czar and his entire family are alive. I am positive of this," was the declaration made to the correspondent today by Michael Chikhachev, a nephew of General Skoropadski, who has just escaped from the Ukraine after a recent trip to Petrograd, Dvinsk, Vilna and Rovno. "I cannot reveal where the Czar is because he does not wish it," he added.

On 18th January 1919 the *New York Times* quoted a British Wireless Service report of a story sent by a special correspondent of the *Morning Post* at Archangel:

> A friend of mine, Prince M–, who has just arrived here from Petrograd, informed me that he had a long talk with the Grand Duke Cyril on November 18th. The Grand Duke told him that he had just received a letter from the Grand Duchess Tatiana, daughter of the Emperor, who wrote that the Empress and her daughters were still alive and that the Emperor had not been shot.

Again, in the *New York Times* on 14th March 1919 was published a report of an interview that had been originally printed in *Giornale d'Italia*, between a woman and Prince Obolensky, in which the Prince expressed his firm belief that the Russian Imperial Family was still alive at that date. He is reported to have refused to give any details as to the basis for his beliefs except that the former Emperor and Empress were, perhaps, hidden in Northern Russia.

On 16th July 1920 there was yet another report about Nicholas, this time in the *San Francisco Examiner*:

APPENDIX

London July 15th. The Soviet Government is offering a reward of 2,000,000 roubles for the head of a man claiming to be Czar Nicholas II of Russia, according to information received by the Jewish Correspondents' Bureau today. The advices say the claimant, who is in Siberia, has raised a considerable following. In accounting for his escape from the hands of the Bolsheviks, he asserts it was a servant impersonating the Czar who was killed at Ekaterinburg, where the Czar and his family are understood to have been executed.

One cannot help noticing the repeated phrases 'It is alleged. . . .', 'It is believed. . . .', 'It is said. . . .', '. . . letters purported to be from. . . .' until one's mind becomes as parched for a direct statement and a true fact as a desert explorer's mouth for a drink of water. But it would seem that there are no facts for us in the desert of *les on-dits*, nor is it ever likely to prove a verdant and fruitful place.

Hopes are momentarily raised by Richard Deacon in his book *A History of the Russian Secret Service*, only to be dashed to the ground once more. On pages 517–518 he writes:

> . . . In recent years some documentary evidence has been circulating of an allegedly successful attempt to rescue the Romanoffs between the middle of 1918 and early 1919. This consists of a series of coded messages of an official kind suggesting an Anglo-American conspiracy to bring the Czar and his family to safety. They have the ring of authenticity, yet would seem to be highly skilled faking of top secret American diplomatic signals. US authorities decline either to deny or confirm their existence. Inquiries in Moscow are met with total silence.

These 'coded messages' obviously refer to what have come to be known as *The Chivers Papers*. These are a

APPENDIX

series of records of wireless messages purported (again!) to have been sent by an American Secret Agent in Siberia in 1918 and 1919 describing the rescue of Nicholas and his family from Ekaterinburg. They tell of a 1,800 mile journey by car and lorry to Odessa and of their embarkation on board a ship of the British Navy. These documents, the existence of which has never been officially confirmed by Washington, were claimed to have been seen, handled and some copied by an ex-member of our parliament who has since disappeared, one Peter Bessell.

Peter Bessell also claimed to have seen, on a visit to the White House, an alleged (once more!) letter from Lord Hardinge to King George V written in 1919 which he copied down. It reads:

Your Majesty,

In response to Your Majesty's enquiry, I have ascertained from the Chargé d'Affaires Vienna that the route taken by His Imperial Majesty the Czar and the Grand Duchesses Olga, Tatiana and Marie was as you were informed by Her Majesty the Queen Mother.

From Odessa to Constantinople arriving February 26,

From Constantinople by train arriving Sofia February 28,

From Sofia to Wien on March 3, arriving Wien March 7,

From Wien to Linz by car arriving March 8,

From Linz to Wroclaw, or Breslau on May 6, arriving Wroclau, May 10.

I am,
Your Majesty's Servant,
Hardinge of P.

APPENDIX

In his latest book, *The Rescue of the Romanovs** Guy Richards goes into all these matters in great detail, and very interesting it all is until one comes to Chapter 17 where he mentions Michael who was purported by some people to have escaped assassination too. He writes that Michael was said to have been 'placed in a home near his son George, both under assumed names somewhere in Europe, and both were visited occasionally by Michael's wife and George's mother, the Countess Brassow. . . .' This is such complete and utter nonsense as to make one doubt the veracity of the rest of Guy Richard's allegations.

Other rumours abounded too about the Imperial family in general, and some of these dated back many years. For instance, there are people who allege that the Empress Alexandra conceived once more, after the birth of Alexis. Others claimed at one time that the Imperial children were removed from the family circle at the age of six and that substitutes were put in their places. During more recent years, since Anna Anderson claimed that she was Anastasia, some people believe that she is truly a Romanoff, but that she is the child of the love-affair between Nicholas and the ballerina Mathilde Kschessinskaya before he married Alexandra. They say that 1894, the year that Anna Anderson gives as the year of her birth, is scarcely mentioned in Kschessinskaya's autobiography; she just glossed over that year by saying that she was ill. So the rumours go on, and on, and on. . . .

The Grand Duke Michael was not immune to rumours either; there were many reports that he too had

---

* Published by The Devin-Adair Company, Old Greenwich, Connecticut, U.S.A., 1975.

APPENDIX

escaped being assassinated. There is in existence a copy of a telegram sent to the Foreign Office in London from the British Representative at Archangel, dated 9th September 1918, which ends:

... I can find no confirmation of presence of Grand Duke Michael in the town though Monsieur Tchaikovski* declared he was here. I should like immediate instructions as to whether he may be despatched with his wife to England if this proves true, and if he desires to go there.

In the minutes of the Shanghai Intelligence Bureau can be found the following entries:

May 15th 1919. HM High Commissioner at Vladivostok has telegraphed to inquire if there is any truth in the report that the Grand Duke Michael, brother of the late Czar, was in Shanghai at the end of March. We stated that though the report was hard to believe, still there was no clear evidence of the Grand Duke's death. As far as is known the rumour is absolutely unfounded. No information whatsoever on the subject being available locally.

May 22nd 1919. HM High Commissioner has further wired that an officer of Semenoff's Army named Suderberg, (at present in Shanghai), and Pfehl, a German officer in Russian Service, were reported to be in touch with the Grand Duke. These officers have not been identified unless they can be Captain Synnerberg and Lt. Pfel. The former is the Russian Commercial Attaché in Shanghai. The latter who arrived in Shanghai bearing a letter of introduction from Colonel Robertson at Vladivostok, stating that he was being sent on a mission to Europe by General Kolchak, was assisted to obtain a passage by SS *Cardiganshire* early in April. Captain Synnerberg and Lt. Pfel are known to be friends but there is no reason to believe that they know anything of Grand Duke Michael.

* Tchaikovski was Chairman/President of the Supreme Council of the Northern Provinces. He had been thrown out by the British but later recalled.

During the years that followed, the rumours seemed to die down slightly, but every now and then would rise again in a newspaper or magazine or even in a book. On 24th August 1927, an article was published in *Le Matin*, written by Henry de Korab, discussing the case of a young man in Poland who was believed by some people to be the Tsarevich Alexis who had escaped from Ekaterinburg. Recently an ex-CIA man wrote a book in which he mentions that in 1959 the Russian experts of the CIA produced a report showing that the Imperial family escaped from Ekaterinburg via Turkestan and China, and finished up in Poland where they died in the 1920s. In 1929 the following report appeared in the *New York Herald Tribune* on Sunday 21st July.

CZAR AND FAMILY STILL ALIVE, COMRADE OF ROYAL AID ASSERTS.

Former Russian Soldier Tells of Visit From Grand Duke's Secretary Who, He Declares, Informed Him of Romanoff Escape by Miracle.

by Frederick Hollowell
By Radio from the Herald Tribune Bureau.
Copyright 1929 New York Herald Tribune.

Rome July 17th. The hope that springs eternal has been revived in the breasts of many exiled Russians by a report which has just come to light here, and which bears many of the ear marks or reliability – to the effect that the former Czar, Czarina and their four daughters and the Czar's brother, Grand Duke Michael Alexandrovitch, are safe and sound, despite the universal belief of long standing that they all perished at the hands of the Bolsheviki during the Red Revolution.

While this is not the first report of such nature since the disappearance of the Russian Imperial family, there appear to be circumstances connected with this one which give a certain element of credence by the very nature of its origin. The report, with supporting evidence, has come to the attention exclusively of the Herald Tribune correspondent through certain 'White' Russian circles here, whose impeccable trustworthiness is beyond question, and is hereby passed on to readers for what it is worth, but with the explanation that it has sufficient basis to sustain unquestioned credibility by numerous exiled Russians living here.

Recounts Visit From Duke's Secretary.
This is the basis of the report: it is generally known that at the time of his disappearance Grand Duke Michael had as private secretary a certain N. N. Johnson, who was always supposed to have suffered the same fate as his employer. Johnson, a Russian of British origin, had as friend and companion before the war Serge Bechtieff, who was a cavalry officer of the Imperial Guard, and who for many years had been living in a small town in Jugoslavia.

Bechtieff has written a long letter, dated June 23, which has circulated among a few exiled Russians in Europe, formally declaring that Johnson, whom he believed long since dead, had suddenly appeared after a decade and paid him a visit in Jugoslavia on February 15 last.

During this visit, Bechtieff declares Johnson swore that he had personal knowledge of the safety of the former Imperial family. Substantiating details are not lacking in Bechtieff's letter, a copy of which has been received by a friend here who showed it to me and who vouched for the writer's honesty of purpose and level-headedness.

Explains Reasons For Prudence.
After rehearsing in his letter many of the supposed circumstances of the kidnapping, murder and burning of the Czar and his family, recounting many known events after that date, and explaining many reasons for prudence in discussing the fate of the Imperial family, Bechtieff continues:

'The hour has struck. My lips are freed from the seal of silence. With inexpressible joy I hasten to impart to all who believe, love and hope for the glad tidings of the mysterious and miraculous rescue of those great martyrs – the family of the Czar. After he had warned me by letter I received at Novig Fontag, Jugoslavia, on February 18 1929, a visit from N. N. Johnson, who I have known many years in Russia and who was private secretary to the Grand Duke Michael Alexandrovitch at the time of the latter's disappearance.'

Reports Whole Family Saved.
It was generally believed they had been kidnapped together and later burned in a furnace near the town of Perm. Johnson told me that His Majesty Czar Nicholas Alexandrovitch, Her Majesty Empress Alexandra Feodorovna, their august daughters Grand Duchesses Olga, Tatiana, Marie and Anastasia and also his Imperial Highness Grand Duke Michael Alexandrovitch are in a word, safe.

The Heir apparent, Prince Alexis Nicholaievich died on February 17 1923 of inflammation of the kidneys. But the whole royal family were saved miraculously after having received the benediction of the Patriarch Tichton who had sent their majesties a replica of the miraculous image of the omnipotent Holy Virgin.

My long conversation with Johnson, whom the world had believed all these years forever lost with the Grand Duke Michael, filled my heart with indescribable joy, for I was fully persuaded that my most cherished dream had at last come true and that my most serene Czar and his august family, as well as the Grand Duke Michael, are alive – as I hereby certify under oath to be a fact.

For many reasons, which the world will understand, I did not ask Johnson where their majesties are at present, in order to avoid the risk of revealing even in chance conversation their whereabouts and thereby unwillingly cause their undoing. Johnson ended his conversation with me in the following words: "Yes, the Czar is alive, and now it depends upon us all whether he shall remount the throne, for it was in response to the prayers of the most faithful sons of our country and after having received the benediction of the most revered patriarch, Tichton, that His Majesty consented to quit his prison and absent himself with his august family and his beloved brother in ascetic solitude, where for many long years he has passed his time praying, working and keeping ceaseless vigil over the welfare of his adored country. More than once His Majesty has expressed his viewpoint by saying that the Russian nation cannot exist outside the Russian frontiers; that the Czar cannot be a part of any emigration and form the head of any one party or political organisation, which would be tantamount to fighting for power. The power of the Czar is given him by God and cannot be acquired either by force or by work of any party. That is why the Czar, with his august family and Grand Duke Michael decided to retire like hermits, and there he will remain, full of hope that the judgement of God will not much longer weigh upon his beloved Russian people and praying for and dreaming of the welfare and rescue of his people until the day when the Russian people shall open their eyes and return to God after throwing off the yoke of slaves of the devil – their oppressors, the Bolsheviki. And if then the Russian people, cured of their blindness, appeal to the Czar he will come with open arms to his well beloved people and consecrate himself to their well being. Therefore, do not extinguish your lamps of faith, do not mourn for those who still live and who will yet save us all. Verily, verily, I beseech you to dry your tears, be of good cheer and full of happiness, for he is very near our gates."

To Bechtieff's letter is added a postscript, saying: 'Let nobody believe this article is meant as an appeal for confirmation of a new party, or the beginning of a fight against any party in existence.' But its sole purpose is to let those who 'love, believe and hope' that those 'whom they adore are still alive.'

Bechtieff explained that he had waited until June to reveal the conversation that took place in Jugoslavia to give ample time for Johnson to return safely to his hiding place, the inference being that Johnson was living with the Imperial family, and judging from the remarks of the Czar quoted by Johnson, they are all living somewhere on Russian soil.

When I consider the possibility that the massacre of the Imperial Family did not take place at the Ipatiev House, and that they escaped eventually to Poland, I admit that I start to wonder. But when I consider the disappearance of the Grand Duke Michael, I do not. There is just a remote possibility that Nicholas and his family may *not* have been done to death in the manner in which is described in history books. But I cannot help feeling that Bykov's account of Michael's death is true. It rings true. Michael vanished, along with Johnson, and Chelycheff, the batman, and Borunov, the chauffeur. They were never seen or heard from again. Natasha heard nothing at all *from* Michael after June 1918, though she heard *of* him many times. The idea that he could have been alive and well as late as 1929, and did not let her know, is to my mind so ridiculous that it is not worth even a passing thought. Had he been alive he would have re-joined her. It might have taken him a long time; it might have been extremely difficult; but even if it had meant crawling the last miles on his hands and knees, he would have managed. I feel that the answer to Michael's disappearance was truthfully described by Bykov, but that the truth of the other mystery has yet to be told. Will we ever know the real answer to the problem which has been described as 'a riddle, wrapped in a mystery, inside an enigma'? Will the riddle ever be solved, the mystery un-wrapped, the enigma undone? We can only hope that one day we will finally be told the answer to one of the most fascinating problems of our times – the mystery of the end of the Romanoffs.

Bibliography

ABRIKOSSOW Dimitri I. *Revelations of a Russian Diplomat.* University of Washington Press, Seattle 1964.
ALEXANDROV Victor. *The End of the Romanovs.* Hutchinson 1966.
Anonymous. *Russian Court Memoirs.* Herbert Jenkins 1917.
BENCKENDORFF Count Paul. *Last Days at Tsarskoe Selo.* Heinemann 1927.
BYKOV Paul. *The Last Days of Tsardom.* Martin Lawrence 1934.
DEACON Richard. *A History of the Russian Secret Service.* Frederick Muller.
KATKOV George. *Russia 1917. The February Revolution.* Longman 1967.
MAJOLIER Nathalie. *Step-daughter of Imperial Russia.* Stanley Paul 1940.
MASSIE Robert K. *Nicholas and Alexandra.* Gollancz 1968.
MIKAILOVITCH Nicholas. *Lettres inédites à Frederick Masson (1914-18).* Payot, Paris 1968.
NABOKOV V. D. *The Provisional Government.* University of Queensland Press, 1971.
PALÉOLOGUE Maurice. *An Ambassador's Memoirs.* Doran 1925.
PARES Sir Bernard. *Fall of the Russian Monarchy,* Cape 1939.

BIBLIOGRAPHY

RICHARDS Guy. *The Hunt for the Czar.* Peter Davies 1971.

RICHARDS Guy. *The Rescue of The Romanovs.* The Devin-Adair Company 1975.

RIVET Charles. *Le dérnier des Romanov.* Paris 1917.

VORRES Ian. *The Last Grand Duchess, The Memoirs of Grand duchess Olga Alexandrovna.* Hutchinson 1964.

WHEATLEY Dennis. *Red Eagle.* Hutchinson 1936 & 1967.

Index

Abakanovitch, Mme, 106
Abrikossov, Dimitri, 7, 8, 41, 42–43, 71, 72
Académie Française, 129
Adlon Hotel, Berlin, 26
Agamemnon, HMS, 113, 132, 160
Alexander II, Tsar of Russia, 47
Alexander III, Tsar of Russia, 13, 15, 16, 48, 49, 50
Alexander Palace, 122
Alexandra Feodorovna, Empress of Russia, 57, 58, 59, 60, 61, 62, 64, 72, 179, 181, 187, 191
Alexandra, Queen of England, 137
Alexaeiev, General Michael Vasilievitch, 73, 86
Alexis, Grand Duke, 34
Alexis Nicholaievitch, Tsarevitch, 17, 34, 35, 56, 62, 65, 70, 73, 75, 181, 182, 187, 189, 191
Alphonso, Ex-King of Spain, 158
Amalienborg Palace, 26
Anastasia Nicholaievna, Grand Duchess, 181, 191
Anastasia, Princess of Montenegro and Duchess of Leuchtenberg, 34
Anderson, Anna, 187
Andrei, Grand Duke, 83
Anichkov Palace, 40, 79
Annenkov, Mlle, 159, 163, 164
Archangel, 188
Arran, Earl of, 136

Bad Kissingen, 36
Balfour, Lord, 131

Ballerup, Denmark, 126
Barnes, G. N., 131
Beard, Charles, 156
Bechtieff, Serge, 190, 192
Belgrade, 124, 129
Beliaiev, General, 73, 74
Benckendorff, Count Paul, 122
Berchtesgaden, 33
Bergen, 39
Berlin, 25, 26
Bescoby-Chambers, John, 180
Blue Cuirassiers, 10, 11, 17, 24
Bolshoi Theatre, 8
Bolton Gardens, Kensington, 144, 157
Bonar Law, 131
Boris Vladimirovitch, Grand Duke, 43, 83, 94, 122
Borunov, (Chauffeur), 121, 193
Brassey, Lady, 114
Brassow, George Mikhailovitch, 31, 32, 33, 36, 96, 134, 144, 145, 147, 148, 149, 150, 152, 153, 164, 165, 166, 187
Brassow, Nathalia Sergeievna, Countess, 4–8 (childhood); 9–11 (1st marriage); 11–12 (2nd marriage); 19–33 (love affair with Michael); 30 (birth of son); 33–35 (marriage to Michael); 36–39 (exile); 39–41 (war time); 41–43 (friendship with Abrikossov); 43–44 (war time); 70, 71, 76; 81–84 (life after Michael's abdication); 85–87 (arrest and liberation); 88, 91, 92, 94, 95, 96, 97; 98–100 (letter from Michael); 101–104 (letter from Michael); 105;

INDEX

106–107 (imprisonment in Cheka);
108–110 (escape to Crimea);
111–112 (Odessa); 113–115 (journey
to England); 119, 120, 122, 130, 131;
134–144 (exile in England); 145, 146,
147, 148; 150–152 (exile in Paris);
152–154 (death of George); 154–158
(financial difficulties); 159–163 (last
years); 163 (illness); 164 (death);
165, 166, 167, 171, 187, 193
Brassowo, 17, 21, 32
Britannia, HMY, 127
Bruevitch, Commissar, 97
Brussels, 52
Bykov, Paul, 120, 123, 179, 180, 183, 193

Canada, 127
Cannes, 36, 37, 148, 149, 152, 160
Cape of Good Hope, 53
Catherine the Great, 24
Chaliapin, 8, 36, 37
Chelicheff, Vassili, 88, 94, 95, 96, 97, 98, 99, 121, 193
Cheremetevskaya, Nathalia Sergeievna, (see Countess Brassow)
Cheremetevskaya, Olga Sergeievna, 4, 7, 8, 9, 40
Cheremetevskaya, Vera Sergeievna, 4, 7, 21, 41
Cheremetevsky, Serge, 21, 81
Chexbres, 25, 27, 29, 36, 38
Christian X, King of Denmark, 123, 124, 125, 126
Constantinople, 77, 113, 124, 160
Cooksville, Canada, 127
Copenhagen, 25, 26, 93, 123, 124, 126
Cotton, Dr., 94, 97, 99, 100
Crimea, the, 88, 91, 111, 124, 183
Cyril, Grand Duke, 34, 64, 82, 147, 151, 184

Davidoff family, 111
Davidson, Colonel, 137
Deacon, Richard, 180, 185
Denikin, General Anton Ivanovitch, 86, 133
Dimitri Constantinovitch, Grand Duke, 129
Dimitri Pavlovitch, Grand Duke, 62
Dolguruki, Prince Vassili, 122

Dostoyevsky, 51, 99
Duma, the, 54, 55, 56, 64, 65, 66, 67, 68, 69, 73, 77

Eastbourne, 133
École des Roches, 146, 148
Eiffel Tower, 38
Ekaterinburg, 103, 107, 122, 123, 124, 177, 178, 179, 180, 181, 182, 183, 185, 189
Elizabeth II, Queen of England, 127
Elizabeth Feodorovna, Grand Duchess, 60
Eristoff, Princess, 151, 154, 164, 166
Eugene, Prince of Leuchtenberg, 34

Fabergé, 126
Filonenko, Captain, 86
Franklin, Mrs, 13, 14, 15
Frant (Sussex), 115
Fredensborg, 15
Froloff, Katia, 25

Galicia, 39, 56
Galitzine, Prince, 73
Galsworthy, John, 131
Gatchina, 11, 12, 18, 29, 39, 40, 41, 42, 70, 71, 72, 73, 81, 82, 83, 85, 87, 88, 92, 100, 101, 104, 105, 107, 108, 120, 122, 127
Geneva, 51
George V, King of England, 124, 125
George Alexandrovitch, Grand Duke, 13, 17
George Mikhailovitch, Grand Duke, 81, 129
Gielgud, Val, 142, 143, 147, 148
Goleniewski, Colonel Michael, 182
Gray, Cecil, 148, 160, 161
Guchkov, Alexander, 68, 69, 70, 78

Hamilton, Lady, 113
Hardinge, Lord, 186
Harrow School, 144, 145, 146
Hennel and Sons, 125
Hesse, Grand Duke of, 34
Hitler, Adolf, 127, 158, 162
Hôtel d'Angleterre, Copenhagen, 26
Hôtel de Londres, Odessa, 111, 112
Hôtel du Parc, Cannes, 36
Hvidore, Denmark, 126

198

INDEX

Ingham, Robert, 182
Ipatiev House, 177, 178, 180, 181, 183, 193
Ireland, 132
Isonzo, SS, 114
Ivan The Terrible, 89

Japan, 52, 53, 54, 73
Johnson, Mme, 115, 119, 120, 137
Johnson, N. N., 40, 70, 74, 81, 83, 86, 87, 94, 96, 99, 101, 106, 115, 120, 121, 190, 191, 193

Karsavina, Tamara, 37
Kazan, University of, 51
Kerensky, Alexander, 50, 66, 68, 69, 75, 76, 78, 85, 86, 87, 88, 90, 91, 122, 128, 129
Khabaloff, General, 66, 74
Kiev, 70, 107, 109, 110, 132
Knebworth, 36, 37, 38, 139, 156
Kolchak, Admiral Alexander, 133, 138, 179, 188
Korea, 52, 54
Korniloff, General, 85, 86
Kosmin, Captain, 84, 85, 87, 88
Kossikovsky, Alexandra, 17
Koulikovsky, Nikolai, 23, 124, 126, 127
Krupskaya, Nadezda, 51
Krymov, General, 65
Kschessinskaya, Mathilde, 187

Lenin, 50, 51, 52, 54, 55, 67, 90, 128, 129, 132
Litchfield, Captain John, 139
Litchfield-Speer, Captain, 113, 134, 136, 137, 139, 140, 141, 145
Liverpool, 39
Lloyd George, 131
London, 51, 114, 125, 126, 148, 155, 160, 163
Lunocharsky, Commissar, 97
Lvov, 40, 70
Lvov, Prince, 68, 69, 73, 79

Madagascar, 53
Majolier, Michael, 160, 161, 163
Malta, 113, 114
Mamontoff, Maroussia, 164
Mamontoff, Nathalie (Tata), 9, 10, 11, 12, 19, 20, 23, 25, 29, 31, 33, 36, 70,
82, 83, 96, 97, 104, 105, 107, 108, 109, 111, 112, 114, 115, 135, 137, 142-144, 147, 148, 149, 150, 155, 157, 158, 160, 161, 162, 163, 164
Mamontoff, Sergei, 8, 9, 10, 11, 12, 130, 143
Manchuria, 52, 54
Marie Feodorovna, Dowager Empress (Mamma), 13, 15, 17, 40, 44, 123, 124, 126, 136, 182
Marie Nicholaievna, Grand Duchess, 181, 191
Markoff, General, 86
Marlborough, HMS, 123
Marlborough House, 137
Marseille, 114
Mary, Queen of England, (May), 126
Marx, Karl, 51
Massie, Robert K., 12, 16
Masson, Frederic, 67, 89, 90, 93
Matveiev, Alexei Sergeievitch, 21, 32, 70, 86, 108, 138
Mensheviks, 52, 67
Methuen, Lord, 114
Michael I, Tsar of Russia, 78
Michael Alexandrovitch, Grand Duke, (Misha), 4, 11, 12; 13-18 (childhood and adolescence); 19-33 (love affair with Natasha); 33-35 (marriage); 36-39 (exile); 39-41 (war time); 41-43 (friendship with Abrikossov); 43-44 (war time); 63, 70; 70-73 (revolutionary stirrings); 75-78 (offered throne); 78-80 (abdication); 81-84 (life after abdication); 85-87 (arrest and release); 88, 91, 92, 93; 94-96 (arrest and exile to Perm); 97-104 (life in Perm); 105, 106, 107, 113, 114, 115; 120-122 (assassination); 124, 127, 138, 139, 140, 144, 150, 154, 155, 156, 157, 165, 166, 168, 169, 170, 171, 172, 176, 187, 188, 189, 190, 191, 192, 193
Michael Mikhailovitch, Grand Duke, 34
Mikhailov Theatre, 43
Milyukov, Paul, 68, 69, 78
Mogilev, 73
Monte Carlo, 36, 37
Moscow, 4, 5, 6, 7, 12, 17, 29, 30, 31, 40, 41, 81, 91, 92, 95, 102, 128, 129

INDEX

Mountbatten, Lord and Lady Louis, 127
Murmansk, 133

Nabokov, V. D., 78, 79, 80, 168, 169, 170, 171
Neame, Miss, 87
Nereide, HMS, 112, 113, 132
Nekrassoff, Nicholas Vissarionovitch, 69, 73, 79
Nevsky Prospekt, 68, 71, 79
New York, 128, 129, 182
Nicholas I, Tsar of Russia, 34, 47
Nicholas II, Tsar of Russia, 4, 13, 22, 33, 34, 47, 49, 52, 53, 54, 55, 56, 57, 65, 66, 67, 68, 69, 70, 71, 73, 74, 75, 80, 82, 122, 123, 168, 169, 171, 177, 179, 181, 182, 183, 184, 185, 186, 187, 189, 190, 191, 192
Nicholas Mikhailovitch, Grand Duke, 61, 67, 68, 71, 82, 89, 90, 91, 93, 129, 130
Nicholas Nicholaievitch, Grand Duke, 57
Nikitine, A. M., 87
Nolde, Baron, 79
Nyanya, 9, 11, 12, 19, 25, 33

Obolensky, Prince, 184
Odessa, 111, 112
Oldenburg, Prince Peter of, 17, 22, 23
Olga Alexandrovna, Grand Duchess, 13, 14, 15, 16, 17, 22, 23, 44, 48, 49, 124, 125, 126, 127, 128, 162
Olga Nicholaievna, Grand Duchess, 181, 191
Omsk, 133
Orcha, 109, 110
Osborne Hotel, Valetta, 114
Otto, Ex-Emperor, 158

Page, Nelson, 183
Paléologue, Maurice, 41, 66, 129, 166
Paris, ix, 38, 67, 89, 114, 129, 145, 147, 148, 149, 150, 153, 154, 157, 159, 162, 164, 165
Passy, Cemetery, ix, 129, 153, 164, 165
Patou, 148
Paul I, Tsar of Russia, 24
Pera Palace Hotel, 113, 134
Percy Lodge, 142, 144, 157

Perm, 95, 96, 97, 98, 101, 104, 105, 120, 121, 122, 181, 191
Petrograd (see also St Petersburg), 40, 56, 65, 66, 67, 68, 70, 73, 78, 81, 82, 85, 86, 88, 89, 91, 92, 93, 96, 100, 101, 105, 106, 109, 110, 121, 126, 129, 169, 179, 184
Philby, Kim, 182
Pleve, Vyacheslav, 52
Pobedonestsev, Constantine Petrovitch, 48
Poland, 56, 181, 189, 193
Ponsonby, Sir Frederick, 125
Port Arthur, 52, 53, 54
Povroskoe, 59, 123
Prinkipo (Büyükada), 124
Pskov, 70
Pushkin, 51
Pushkino, 7, 100
Putyatin, Prince and Princess, 70, 74, 76, 78, 79, 92, 95

Rasputin, Gregory Efimovitch, 58, 59–64, 71, 72, 123, 128
Richards, Guy, 187
Riga, Treaty of, 154
Rodzyanko, Michael, 66, 73, 74, 75, 78, 79, 80, 129
Rovno, 44, 184
Rozdestvensky, Admiral, 53
Rumania, 111
Russian Social Democratic Workers Party, 52, 54
Russo-Japanese War, 52–53

St Geneviève-des-Bois, 164, 165
St Leonards-on-Sea College, 135
St Moritz, 37
St Petersburg (see also Petrograd), 11, 24, 33, 39, 41, 50, 51, 56, 62, 167
Savinkoff, Boris Victorovitch, 84
Sens, 153
Sergius, Grand Duke, 54
Seroff, Commissar, 105, 107, 108
Sèvres-Babylone, 159
Shanghai, 188
Shaw, G. B., 131
Shulgin, Basil, 70, 78
Shleiffer, 40
Siberia, 47, 51, 59, 61, 64, 91, 128, 138, 185, 186

INDEX

Simbirsk, 50
Simpson, Mrs, 4
Sinn Fein, 132
Skirmisher, HMS, 113
Smolny Institute, 92, 94
Snape, 115, 134, 139, 140, 142, 157
Sokolov, Nicholas, 179, 180, 181
Sorbonne, La, 148
Stalin, Joseph, 127, 162
Svistunov, Captain, 84, 85

Tallinn, 130
Tata, see Mamontoff, Nathalie Sergeievna,
Tatiana Nicholaievna, Grand Duchess, 181, 184, 191
Tereschenko, Michael Ivanovitch, 68, 69, 87
Thorpe, Jeremy, 177
Tobolsk, 59, 122, 123, 179
Tolstoy, Leo, 51
Tolstoy, Prince and Princess, 70
Troitski, Mr, 14
Trotsky, Leon, 55, 90, 128
Tsarski Sad, 24
Tsarskoe Selo, 40, 44, 83
Tsushima, Straits of, 53
Tukine, M. and Mme, 145
Tunbridge Wells, 115
Turgenev, 51

Udinka, 30, 31
Ukraine, the, 109, 110, 139, 184
Ulyanov, Alexander, 50, 51
Ulyanov, Vladimir Ilyitch, see Lenin
Ulster, 132
Uritsky, Commissar, 93, 94, 95, 97, 98, 106, 108, 120, 129

Vedikhoff, 86
Venus, SS, 39
Verderevsky, Dimitri Nikolaievitch, 87
Versailles, Conference, 131
Veshinsky, 87
Vestfalen, Professor, 87
Victoria-Melita, Grand Duchess, 34, 64
Victoria, Princess, 137
Vienna, 25, 33
Vladivostok, 133, 188
Vologda, 96, 129

Wadhurst, 115
Wales, Edward, Prince of, 4
Wells, H. G., 131
Wiasemsky, Princess, 97, 105, 108, 109, 111, 112, 115, 137
Wilton, Robert, 179
Wimbledon, 142
Windsor, 11
Winter Palace, 48, 54, 56, 74, 90, 91
Witte, Count Sergius, 53, 54, 55
Wulfert, Liolocha, 10, 11, 20, 21, 25, 32, 33, 35

Xenia Alexandrovna, Grand Duchess, 13, 124, 125, 126, 128, 137

Yachontoff, Mme, 109
Yalu Timber Company, 52
Youssoupoff, Prince Felix, 62, 63, 128, 163
Yusefovitch, General, 81

Zina, Princess, 34
Znamerovsky, 99